“Did you c … ?”

Words spilled from Dr. Orande’s mouth. “I am under official orders not to—”

“The report, Doctor,” Mack Bolan growled. “Where is it?”

Orande began to perspire, despite the chill of the morgue. His shaking hands retrieved keys from a coat pocket. With difficulty he fit the key into the file cabinet lock and opened it. Then he pulled out a folder and handed it to the Executioner, who studied the report inside. The doctor had found five 9 mm slugs lodged in vital organs.

Bolan forced the small man to lead the way out of the morgue and up the stairs to the lobby. Then the pair walked through the main doors.

“Wait fifteen minutes before you call anybody,” Bolan ordered, then added, “I can always come back.”

As he vanished into the shadows, the Executioner knew he was about to make Major Pieter Volksmann’s life hell.

MACK BOLAN®

The Executioner

#152 Combat Stretch
#153 Firebase Florida
#154 Night Hit
#155 Hawaiian Heat
#156 Phantom Force
#157 Cayman Strike
#158 Firing Line
#159 Steel and Flame
#160 Storm Warning
#161 Eye of the Storm
#162 Colors of Hell
#163 Warrior's Edge
#164 Death Trail
#165 Fire Sweep
#166 Assassin's Creed
#167 Double Action
#168 Blood Price
#169 White Heat
#170 Baja Blitz
#171 Deadly Force
#172 Fast Strike
#173 Capitol Hit
#174 Battle Plan
#175 Battle Ground
#176 Ransom Run
#177 Evil Code
#178 Black Hand
#179 War Hammer
#180 Force Down
#181 Shifting Target
#182 Lethal Agent
#183 Clean Sweep
#184 Death Warrant
#185 Sudden Fury
#186 Fire Burst
#187 Cleansing Flame
#188 War Paint
#189 Wellfire
#190 Killing Range
#191 Extreme Force
#192 Maximum Impact
#193 Hostile Action
#194 Deadly Contest
#195 Select Fire
#196 Triburst
#197 Armed Force
#198 Shoot Down
#199 Rogue Agent
#200 Crisis Point
#201 Prime Target
#202 Combat Zone
#203 Hard Contact
#204 Rescue Run
#205 Hell Road
#206 Hunting Cry
#207 Freedom Strike

DON PENDLETON'S

THE EXECUTIONER®

FREEDOM STRIKE

A GOLD EAGLE BOOK FROM
WORLDWIDE®

TORONTO • NEW YORK • LONDON
AMSTERDAM • PARIS • SYDNEY • HAMBURG
STOCKHOLM • ATHENS • TOKYO • MILAN
MADRID • WARSAW • BUDAPEST • AUCKLAND

First edition March 1996
ISBN 0-373-64207-5

Special thanks and acknowledgment to
David North for his contribution to this work.

FREEDOM STRIKE

Printed in U.S.A.

No evil is honorable: but death is honorable;
therefore death is not evil.

—Zeno
B.C. 335–264

In peace sons bury their fathers.
In war fathers bury their sons.

—Sir Francis Bacon
1561–1626

It's about time people stood up to be counted for what they believe in. Otherwise, the only time they'll be counted is as casualties of war.

—Mack Bolan

To those who strive to throw off oppression's yoke

1

Pretoria, South Africa

Night was approaching, but the heat of the waning sun still made the young black man sweat. Something else made him shiver. Kenny Mgabe knew it was his time to die.

Through eyes swollen by constant beatings, the young man glanced at his uniformed executioner. The Bureau of State Security major sat behind the wheel of the parked police vehicle, looking through the windshield at the huge structure ahead.

He turned his head and stared out a window of the car at the blossoming jacaranda trees that lined the long driveway. Ahead of him was the huge Boer monument that sat on the edge of Pretoria, South Africa's administrative capital.

The tropical trees reminded him of the jacarandas he and his sister, Sonda, had seen in Mexico City the previous spring. The two of them had gone there for a brief vacation after graduating from university in the U.S., and before returning to South Africa.

It was strange that he would think about Mexico City and jacarandas now, as if he wanted to remember everything good that had happened to him before dying, such as helping to elect the first black president of South Africa. It seemed like a lifetime had passed, but he knew it was really not that long ago since the election.

He also felt satisfaction at seeing the bigots—white and black—lose their power as apartheid, the policy of strict racial segregation that had been imposed on blacks and other people of color, became only an ugly memory with the president's election.

He thought about Sonda again. So much had changed when they returned. For one thing, he had.

There was a time when all they thought about was getting a Zulu elected president. Their heritage was Zulu, and from the time they were children they had heard stories about the great Zulu warriors of the past. As teenagers, his sister had dragged him to lectures about the history of their tribe, given by Dr. Abel Methabane. The medical man was also a Zulu activist.

Kenny had found him out of touch with reality, but Sonda worshiped him. He didn't think his sister or her mentor had ever forgiven him for questioning that a Zulu was destined to lead South Africa. Or that he had gone to work as a speech writer for the first black presidential candidate of South Africa, Nelson Mandela, someone who wasn't a Zulu.

While he had spent his time in the U.S. studying history, philosophy and ethics, Sonda had spent every minute away from classes, learning about weapons and competing at shooting competitions.

As she had told him many times, somebody in their family had to carry on the tradition of the Zulu warrior. It no longer interested him, so she had decided she would.

When she joined him, as part of the security team protecting the new president after the elections, he thought she had changed her attitude. Then he realized she hadn't.

He still remembered their first serious argument.

"Did you take the job to protect the new president, or to be close enough to kill him?"

She had become furious that he would question her motives.

"Perhaps you should have gotten a job with the Inkatha Freedom Party instead of with the new government," he suggested.

"The Inkathas are politicians. We are Zulus," she snapped.

"The time to win battles with spears is over. Even your Zulu activist friends have to admit that the people voted for the president because he was the right man. Not because he belonged to a particular tribe."

He remembered how angry she had been when she stormed out of his flat. He hadn't realized that her anger extended to all whites until the previous day, when he told her that he had asked for help from the United States government. She'd become furious when he told her that a reporter from an American news service was coming to South Africa to meet with him. The newsman wanted to write a story to expose the key government and business officials who were secretly backing terrorist groups still trying to destroy the new government before it could impose a new philosophy of hope and equality on the country.

She had asked him if that included black groups.

"All groups," he replied.

"I suppose this reporter is white," she snapped.

"Does it matter?"

"To me, it does."

"Don't forget it was a white man who paid for your university education," he reminded her.

"Harry Desmond wanted something in return," she replied in anger.

"What?"

Sonda had to stop and think. "Probably the free publicity he got for giving two poor blacks free scholarships," she replied sarcastically.

KENNY STILL DIDN'T ANSWER his phone. Sonda Mgabe was getting worried.

Pushing a package of cigarettes into her shoulder bag, she reviewed her evening schedule. Two meetings were scheduled, both with Zulu activist groups. But she planned to stop by Kenny's apartment in Pretoria to make sure he was all right before she returned to Johannesburg.

The Bureau of State Security—BOSS—had been keeping a close watch on both of them. Even though she resented it, Sonda understood why. Kenny and she had become role models for the young blacks of South Africa, who could dare hope to go to college and become something more than servants, miners or mindless laborers.

BOSS was under fire from the new government for its past activities—especially those involving the intimidation of blacks and the white liberals who supported them. Its agents were nothing more than thugs, using guns and clubs to kill or beat confessions out of those they arrested. The agency had shrunk in size and authority, although its leaders seemed to operate as if the old government were still in power.

Sonda blamed Harry Desmond and his hunger for publicity for their predicament. She'd complained to Dr. Methabane about constantly being annoyed by television and newspaper reporters. Gently he had reminded her that every gift had a price tag.

"Mr. Desmond isn't a bad sort for a white man. He's like one of those benevolent slave owners who prided himself on providing his blacks with the best of everything...except freedom and dignity."

The doctor was right. Desmond was probably not "a bad sort," as Dr. Methabane had put it. She only hoped he would find some new toys to brag about to the press and leave them alone.

It was Kenny, not Desmond, who was playing right into the hands of the security police by meeting the white reporter from the United States. Knowing how BOSS operated, Sonda was certain that they didn't care that her brother was with the government. They would find some excuse to drag him into one of their private interrogation rooms and force him to reveal what he was planning to tell the American reporter. And nobody would know they had questioned him until they decided to let him go.

After their fight, it had seemed sensible to call Dr. Methabane and ask him for advice. As head of the Zulu Action Front, she was sure that the wise doctor could suggest how to help her brother not get entwined in the security police web.

The doctor had told her Kenny had to make his own decisions. She couldn't interfere with that, any more than she would want Kenny interfering in her affairs. She knew the doctor was right. Still, she couldn't help worrying.

A female voice startled her. "How about a drink?"

Naomi Markus, a young white volunteer from Cape Town, stood in the open doorway.

Sonda looked up and shook her head. "I've got two meetings tonight." Then she remembered her concern about her brother. "Actually three. I want to run up to Pretoria and stop by Kenny's place for a moment."

"Tomorrow?"

"Sounds good to me," Sonda replied, then reached down and picked up her overstuffed attaché case.

Naomi walked away while Sonda checked her purse.

The pistol was still there, loaded and ready to fire. She didn't think she'd need to use the 9 mm Heckler & Koch P-7 M-8, but she was prepared for anything.

MGABE COULD FEEL THE HATE of the tall security police major sitting next to him, and he wondered how and when Major Pieter Volksmann would kill him.

Volksmann's men had almost succeeded in accomplishing that with the continual beatings they'd administered.

They hadn't bothered to show him identification when they'd picked him up after work as he walked to his car.

Instead of taking him to the central police station, they had taken him to a small brick building on King George Street. He wasn't sure if they really were BOSS agents. All he knew was that he would probably never leave the brick building alive.

Something still confused Kenny. If Volksmann was planning to kill him, why was he taking him to the monument? He looked at the huge structure that rose at the end of the driveway.

The Voortrekker Monument was a tribute to the Dutch settlers who had enslaved the southern portion of the African continent.

A stone wall carved with sixty-four ox wagons in a circle surrounded the huge, cubelike structure. He could see the carved head of a Cape buffalo, considered by many to be the most dangerous of all African animals, hanging above the large entrance.

Volksmann turned to his prisoner and spoke the first words he had uttered since they'd left central Pretoria.

In a thick Afrikaans accent, he waved a hand at the huge stone complex and said, "Magnificent, isn't it?"

Mgabe shrugged. He glanced at the short metal-studded baton the police major held in his hand and decided to keep quiet. The one thing he was sure about was that even the most innocuous answer would result in a blow from the baton.

"Do you know where we are?"

The young man nodded his head.

"If only you savages would understand that we Boers are the real chosen people. Imagine! A handful of pioneers, disgusted at the British deciding to make everyone equal—even you black animals. So they packed their families into ox-drawn wagons and began a journey across South Africa that became an example for all decent white men since. We, the Voortrekkers, were protected by God, even more than the Jews of the Old Testament! Or weren't you taught about the Battle of Blood River?"

Mgabe knew the story of the Voortrekkers. Like every South African student, white and black, he'd been forced by government-subsidized teachers to memorize the story.

The complex was dedicated to the memory of those Dutch immigrants who had traveled north over the coastal mountains of the Cape and into the heart of the veld. The Battle of Blood River, fought on December 16, 1838, had been beaten into his memory by repetition from his teachers.

Under the leadership of Andries Pretorius, for whom the capital of the Transvaal Province was named, a handful of Boers—470 of them—fought a battle with twelve thousand Zulu warriors. More than three thousand of the warriors were killed, while only three of the Trekkers received any kind of wound.

"They talked about it in school," Mgabe replied in a flat tone. "Of course, the Dutch had guns, and all the Zulu warriors had were spears."

His reply was rewarded with a slash of the baton, which opened a deep gash on the edge of his right cheek. Mgabe didn't care. In his veins flowed the blood of Zulu warriors. He wondered if the police major knew that. He didn't think so. Even if he did, the young man was positive he didn't care.

Volksmann wanted something else from him. Mgabe wasn't sure what it was, but he knew the security cop would tell him when the time came.

He remembered when the major had entered the interrogation room earlier that evening. He had asked the man why he was being held. His question had earned him a blow from the baton Volksmann held in his hand.

He would have tried to fight back, even if it cost him his life, except that manacles pinned his arms behind him.

The big blond cop had glared at him. "There is nothing you can do for or to us, kaffir," he shouted. "Do you know who I am?"

Mgabe nodded. He knew. Volksmann's face had appeared on television and on the front pages of newspapers. By reputation he was probably the second or third most powerful man in the security police organization. According to the newspapers, the BOSS major was about fifty, unmarried, had come from a small all-white town in Northern Transvaal and had been with the police for more than twenty-five years.

"Do you know why you are here?"

Mgabe shook his head.

"You've been charged with acts of terrorism."

There was no point in arguing with Volksmann. He'd only get another beating with the baton.

The security official confronted the young man with a shouted question. "Do you deny you are a terrorist?"

Mgabe started to argue, but the major stopped him.

"This American you were meeting tonight—is he bringing you money so you can continue your activities?"

He started to explain.

"Don't bother lying," Volksmann snapped.

The major forced him to his feet. "Come. I want you to see why you and your fellow terrorists can never destroy us, no matter who or how much money you have backing you."

They had driven to the monument, and Mgabe wondered if this was what the BOSS officer wanted him to see. He was confused. This wasn't a black man's monument.

Without explanation, the major opened his car door and got out, carefully gripping the 9 mm SIG-Sauer P-226 in his right hand, then walked around the car and opened the door on the passenger side.

"Walk in front of me," he ordered as he reached inside the car and retrieved a canvas musette bag.

Kenny moved unsteadily up the walkway, hampered by the heavy manacles on his wrists and ankles. His body still quivered from the barrage of beatings it had sustained throughout the night.

They walked down a short flight of stairs and stopped in front of a dirt-covered metal door.

"Open it!"

Volksmann pushed the young man inside and forced him to walk down a musty-smelling corridor.

Mgabe felt the barrel of the automatic pistol jab into the small of his back.

"Stop!"

The young man looked around. The ceiling above was raised. He wondered if this spot was where he would die.

He turned to Volksmann. "What time is it?"

The security police official seemed amused at the question. "Late for a date?"

Mgabe was. He was supposed to meet the reporter at his flat that night.

The major interrupted his prisoner's private thoughts. "I have sent some men to pick up your American contact."

Volksmann smiled coldly.

"Meantime, you are about to perform a great service for your kaffir president." He waved his hand at the ceiling. "Above where we are standing is the center of the Voortrekker Monument. You are about to blow it up."

Mgabe stared at the major. What game was he playing now?

Volksmann continued to smile. "Of course, you can't do anything with your hands behind your back." He took out a key chain, then moved before the young man and removed the handcuffs and leg irons.

Mgabe gently massaged his chafed wrists, while the major reached into the musette bag he was carrying and took out a quarter-pound block of gray white material that looked like clay. Attached to it was a timing device.

Keeping a watchful eye on his prisoner, the major placed the device against the wall and started the clock.

Now Mgabe understood Volksmann's plan: blow up the monument and plant evidence that black terrorists had been responsible. It would destroy the new president's claim that his government cared about all South African citizens, especially if they found the body of one of his staff members in the rubble.

He could hear the security police major at the press conference:

His name was Kenneth Mgabe. He worked for the new government. Obviously he wasn't very knowledgeable about handling explosives. The decent people of South Africa are fortunate that the dead man didn't know how much explosive was needed to destroy our hallowed monument. As it is, the damage is extensive and will require major repairs.

And because of him, the new government would lose support from the whites who had voted for it.

Rage suddenly consumed the young man. He'd returned to South Africa to help save his country, not destroy it. And now he was going to die. Perhaps he could stop Volksmann first. He jumped at the security police major, then saw the silenced automatic pistol in his hand.

The major pulled the trigger and fired at the young man's chest, the impact of the bullet spinning Mgabe.

He could feel the burning inside, but the adrenaline of revenge kept him moving toward the major.

Again and again Volksmann fired, each round drilling a hole in Mgabe's chest or stomach.

Once more he reached his arms out to grab the major, but fell, facedown, on the cold, damp floor in a pool of his blood.

Volksmann moved to the still-quivering form on the ground and fired a final shot into the carotid artery. He turned from the body and knelt to check the detonator clock.

"Three minutes to go," he muttered. "Time to leave. It wouldn't do to have my body found here, too."

Quickly he walked back down the corridor and out the metal door.

Driving away from the monument, Volksmann began to whistle a melody he hadn't thought of since his childhood. His men would take care of Mgabe's visitor.

And his foreign bank account would get a little fatter.

A muted explosion reached his ears as he headed back to central Pretoria. Time to change into a clean uniform and get ready to investigate the outrageous attempt to blow up the sacred Voortrekker Monument.

2

Something was wrong.

The contact hadn't shown up yet. He was thirty minutes late by the warrior's calculations. Mack Bolan, a.k.a. the Executioner, wondered if he had changed his mind.

The big American was annoyed. The flight from New York had taken the better part of a day, with a plane change in London. As soon as he landed at Jan Smuts International Airport, located roughly between Pretoria and Johannesburg, he had rented an Audi 500.

He'd driven thirty-five minutes north to Pretoria on the N1 freeway, then switched to the N4 freeway and continued driving until he reached Atteridgeville.

Weaving his way through the garbage-laden roads that crisscrossed the segregated community, he searched until he finally found the apartment complex.

The warrior knew that Atteridgeville, like most black townships, was crowded with poverty-stricken blacks. Forced by previous governments to live in ghettos that were more like concentration camps than communities the residents had to endure conditions reminiscent of the days of Nazi dictator Adolph Hitler. Bolan could sense their anger and distrust when they saw a white face.

Not that he blamed them.

But he knew it took time to get rid of more than three hundred years of hate and prejudice. Progress wouldn't come overnight. This was the first time in South African history that someone other than a white was running the country.

Bolan had hidden the Audi behind a row of trash Dumpsters. The shadows from the huge containers made his vehicle almost invisible. And from his vantage point, he had a clear view of the steps that led up to his contact's second-floor apartment.

Nobody had answered when he rapped on the door to apartment 201, and none of the apartment lights were on.

He'd return to the car, wait another thirty minutes, then leave.

Back at the car, he started feeling travel fatigue from the long flight. Slouched down in his seat behind the wheel of the rented car, he let his eyes close. At least he could get a little rest until the contact showed up, or he gave up in disgust and left.

EXCEPT FOR THE HANDFUL of staffers who were required to be on duty overnight, the American Embassy was nearly empty.

A tall, conservatively dressed young man stopped at the small coffee bar, filled his cup, then returned to his office and closed the door.

A stack of official documents waited for him. They had to be digested, initialed, reviewed with his boss and turned over to the crypto section for coding and transmission to Langley.

There was also the thick, sealed package from Kenny Mgabe, who had asked if he would hold it for him.

Jay Preston sat at his desk, ignoring the package and pile of papers, and wondered how the meeting between Kenny Mgabe and the man from Washington was going.

He had stuck his neck out for Kenny and made some calls to Washington, D.C. Mgabe and his people needed help to stop the neofascist terrorist groups from trying to overthrow the new integrated government.

Preston had called Mgabe early that morning to alert him that a man was on his way to South Africa.

"Just one man?" Mgabe had sounded disappointed. "Who is he?"

"A reporter named Mike Belasko. My contact says he's good."

"A reporter? I was hoping the American government would send a platoon of jungle fighters to wipe out the right-wing hit squads."

"We can't get involved officially. But meet him, Kenny," Preston urged. "He's supposed to be...*special.*"

"Other reporters have come here and written about our troubles," Mgabe replied in disgust. "But I'll meet him."

"Good. I gave him your home address. He'll come straight from Jan Smuts airport. Around eight tonight."

"At least he isn't some professional killer from your CIA."

The young government field officer had winced at the comment. He wasn't a professional killer, but he did work for the Agency.

The door to his office opened and the young, dark-haired woman who worked for him entered. She handed him a videotape.

"This was just broadcast. A news bulletin."

He studied the tape, puzzled. "What about?"

Her face was expressionless as she stated, "Kenneth Mgabe is dead."

BOLAN OPENED HIS EYES and looked around, noting that there was one new car in the parking area. Then he glanced up at the second floor.

Behind drawn shades he could see that the lights in his contact's apartment were lit. He wondered if the man had returned home while he was dozing.

He looked up at the windows again and saw the shadows of three forms reflected on the shades.

His keen ears picked up the muted sounds of banging from inside the upper-floor apartment. They were familiar noises. The three intruders were tearing the apartment apart, and Bolan wondered if his contact was in there with them.

Bolan glanced at the bag sitting next to him, on the passenger seat of the Audi.

Hal Brognola had shipped the canvas carryall to the American Embassy in Pretoria via an Air Force cargo jet. The bag, containing the Executioner's battle gear, had been delivered to him by a young woman from the embassy after he cleared customs.

From the bag he retrieved a 9 mm Beretta 93-R, with a modified Invicta suppressor threaded onto the barrel. Then the big man slipped into a shoulder-holster rig and leathered the automatic. A .44 Magnum Desert Eagle fit snugly into the holster he slid through his wide belt and centered at the small of his back. Around his forearm he strapped the sheath that held his third weapon, a razor-sharp Ka-bar combat knife.

After slipping several extra clips into his jacket pocket, Bolan hurried to the recently arrived vehicle, a large black car that most likely had transported the three hardmen.

Glancing inside, he could see that the interior rear-door handles were missing, as were the window handles. The intruders upstairs were either security police or hit men from some local criminal element.

The Executioner knew a lot about the South African security agency. The Bureau of State Security protected the country from espionage and terrorist incidents. At least that was what its mandate claimed. From what Brognola had told him, BOSS's real job was to get rid of anybody who disagreed with its racist policies.

The agents they employed were bigots who knew how to beat information out of the people they took into custody—sometimes to the point of torturing them until they died, or killing them and placing the blame for their deaths elsewhere.

Supposedly the most brutal of their agents had already been dismissed. Only a handful were still officially on the agency's payroll. But Bolan knew that if they were anything like the secret police of other countries, the leaders of BOSS had found ways to keep using their thugs.

He studied the grounds around the two-story buildings. No one seemed to be standing guard.

It was time for Bolan to find out who the intruders were and why they were there.

He unleathered the Beretta, flicked the fire selector to burst mode, then mounted the exterior steps to the second floor. For a brief moment he listened at the door to apartment 201. He could hear banging noises from inside.

Without hesitation, he slammed his shoulder against the apartment door, the force of his assault tearing the door from the wooden frame. He burst across the threshold, taking in at a glance the scene in the small living room. Three men, with the hard expressions of street professionals, knelt on the floor, sorting through the piles of clothing and papers they had dumped there.

The closest hardman started to scramble to his feet, attempting to unleather a SIG-Sauer P-226 from its hip holster.

Bolan had the Beretta up and ready, drilling him with a pair of well-placed rounds. The force of the impacts drove the man backward two steps, then he collapsed to the floor.

The other two hardmen leaped to their feet, grabbing for the automatic pistols in their hip holsters, and fired at Bolan's position.

The Executioner was no longer there. As soon as he'd unleashed his first two rounds, he shifted position to face his other two targets.

The second hardman had succeeded in unleashing a round from his Glock 17, but the hastily triggered slug flew wide of its mark. Before the guy could pull the trigger again, Bolan's Beretta quietly coughed twice.

The hardman took the pair of slugs just above his right eye. He backpedaled furiously, trying to stand on his feet, but gravity, and death, took over and he crashed to the floor.

Bolan quickly swung left to face the remaining intruder. The hardman fired his SIG-Sauer P-226, but the Executioner was already on the move. The soft-nosed 9 mm projectile missed him, instead shattering a framed photograph of an elderly black couple.

The big American fired two shots into his adversary, both rounds chewing into the man's sternum.

Still standing despite the two chest wounds, the hardman tried desperately to line up the Executioner in his sights.

Bolan turned his Beretta a fraction to the right and fired a round that tore into the gunner's stomach.

Cursing, the hardman forced his hand to pull the trigger one last time. The slug tore into the floor, and the gunman collapsed on top of it.

His eyes were still blinking when Bolan knelt next to him. "What were you looking for?"

The hardman forced a weak smile. "You, Belasko. We don't like kaffir lovers...." He gasped for air.

"Where's the man who lives here?"

The intruder smiled grimly. "Waiting for you to join him."

"Who sent you?"

There was no reply. The gunman's smile and eyes were frozen in death.

Bolan checked the other two men. They were dead, as well.

He had one question. How did the gunners know his name?

He looked at the mess of clothing and paper on the floor. The man who lived here was supposed to have collected evidence about the backers of the terrorist groups.

Where was it? And where was his contact?

As his eyes searched the room for a likely hiding place for the promised evidence, Bolan thought back to the conversation he'd had with Hal Brognola at Stony Man Farm—the United States's top secret counterterrorist installation—two days earlier. The big Fed had asked him to do everything he could to keep South Africa's first black president from being assassinated.

"You're not going there to influence the people," Brognola reminded him as he chomped on an unlit cigar. "That was decided by the voters on election day. Just make sure the different hate gangs don't get together to assassinate the man most of the South Africans wanted to run the country." He paused to let the thought sink in. "Got any ideas on how to handle the situation?"

"Not yet. I suppose the first step is to get the terrorist groups distrusting one another." He looked at his old friend. "It may turn into a bloodbath."

"It already has," Brognola commented. "Between the right-wing white terrorist groups like the Afrikaner Weerstandsbeweging, the White Wolves, the Orde van die Dood, and the fanatic black movements like the Anzanian People's Liberation Army, the Zulu Action Front and a whole bunch of tiny white and black militant groups, you've got a giant powder keg about to explode, blasting the country back to where it was before the election."

Having been to South Africa before, Bolan understood. He knew a lot about the Afrikaner Weerstandsbeweging—the Afrikaner Resistance Movement. It was the largest of the paramilitary groups and was widely known under the acronym AWB. Orde van die Dood—Order of Death—like all of the white neofascist gangs, was populated with fanatics who claimed to be willing to die to keep the blacks from power.

The Executioner wasn't as familiar with the black terrorist organizations.

The big Fed explained them.

"The Azanian Army is the paramilitary branch of the Pan Africanist Congress, which wants to kick all the whites out of Africa. And, despite its name, the Zulu Action Front is not affiliated with the Inkatha Freedom Party, but had demanded that a Zulu be made president. Election or no election. All of them wanted the right man to get into office and are ticked off that he didn't."

"And the only right man was the one each group backed."

The head Fed nodded. "Sounds hopeless, doesn't it?" He didn't wait for Bolan's reply. "That's what I told the man at 1600 Pennsylvania when he brought up the subject."

"You'd have to be crazy to think you could make a difference," Bolan agreed.

Because Bolan wasn't on the payroll of the United States government, all the top Fed could do was ask for his help. But the Executioner had yet to turn down his old friend when he asked for assistance.

"The Man thinks you can make a difference."

"It sounds like a civil war is about to break out," Bolan replied.

"You might be right. Most of the terrorist groups have warehouses filled with guns." Brognola handed Bolan several sheets of paper. "Here are the storage places we know about. There are more."

"Who's paying their bills?"

"The man you'll be meeting with when you get to South Africa claims he has the names of the more important backers of the various groups trying to destroy the new government. And hard evidence to back up his claims.

"His name is Kenneth Mgabe. He and his sister went to university here on scholarships. They graduated last spring."

"They sound like a couple of bright kids," Bolan commented.

"They must have been. One of the richest men in South Africa, Harry Desmond, paid their tuition."

"They work for him now?"

"No. Both of them work for the government—the new government."

"I guess it wouldn't do any harm to fly down and have a talk with Kenneth Mgabe," Bolan said casually. "See what he's got."

"Especially if you're a reporter for some big American news syndicate looking for a scoop." The big Fed dropped a press card made out to Mike Belasko on the desk, along with a matching passport.

As he mentally reviewed the conversation with Hal Brognola, Bolan kept searching the room. There was nothing on the floor that resembled the evidence he'd been promised. He looked behind the framed prints and photographs on the living-room wall and came up empty.

Perhaps the documents were hidden in the bedroom or on the rear balcony. Bolan started to get up, wondering if he would find Kenneth Mgabe's body back there, too.

As Bolan slipped the Beretta back in its shoulder rig, he felt the cold circle of a muzzle against the back of his neck and heard an icy female voice, speaking with a South African accent.

"Who are you and where is my brother?"

3

The Executioner kept a firm grip on the Beretta. Few of his adversaries had ever been able to get the upper hand, and he didn't intend to add this woman to the list.

Possible options for overcoming the woman holding the gun flashed through his mind in mere seconds, all of them seeming to end in the same way—with his death.

He'd have to rely on the facts and hope that she'd believe him.

"I came here to meet your brother at his invitation. Who are you?"

"His sister, Sonda. You have an American accent," the woman replied. "Are you the American reporter he was supposed to meet?"

Bolan nodded, feeling the muzzle of the weapon moving with him.

"Turn around."

Bolan did.

A young black woman pointed a Heckler & Koch P-7 M-8 at him. Bolan recognized the weapon. He knew it was a deadly tool in the hands of a skilled enemy.

The woman who held it steady was as close to a real beauty as he had seen in a long time. She was tall and slim, with legs that seemed to continue forever.

Except for her face. The fury and distrust she felt were reflected in her features. Instinctively the large man knew she could be a dangerous opponent. The woman looked as if she could kill without shame or guilt. And from the confident way she handled the 9 mm pistol, she knew how to do it expertly.

She looked at the three still-bleeding corpses in disdain, then back at him. "Did you bring those three?"

"No," he replied. "They were here when I arrived. And I don't know where your brother is. I was too busy to worry about him."

"For a reporter you seem to know how to handle a gun."

Bolan hoped his reply would satisfy her. "Tools of the trade for a place like South Africa."

She nodded in agreement.

"We ought to get out of here before somebody calls the cops," he added.

"There are too many killed every night in Atteridgeville for anyone to think something special is going on." She held out her free hand. "Your gun."

Bolan reluctantly handed the Beretta to her, butt first. He felt reassured, knowing the .44 Magnum Desert Eagle was holstered against the small of his back.

"Walk ahead of me," she ordered.

He led the way into the small bedroom. Like the living room, clothing and papers were scattered everywhere. But there was no sign of the young man he was supposed to meet.

Sonda backed her way to a small glass door and opened it. Quickly she glanced outside. Before Bolan could grab her, she turned back.

"He's not out there," she said, sounding relieved. "What did Kenny have that made you come all the way to South Africa?"

"Hard evidence about who was funding the various terrorist groups."

She looked surprised, then prodded him to return to the living room. The telephone rang as the two of them entered the ransacked room. Keeping her eyes focused on Bolan, Sonda Mgabe picked up the receiver.

As she listened to the voice on the other end, her features tightened. Pools of tears welled up in her eyes, then began to run down her cheeks. To Bolan, it looked as if somebody had just stabbed her with a knife.

"Thanks for telling me, Naomi," she said, and hung up.

Ignoring the large man who stood before her, she walked over to the small television sitting on a low bookcase and turned it on.

A newscaster was talking. Bolan couldn't understand the Afrikaans words he was using, until the body of a young black man partially covered by rubble was shown. The television reporter gave a name to the body—Kenneth Mgabe.

Footage of the results of the bombing were shown. To Bolan's trained eyes, the actual damage seemed minor, as if the dead man didn't know how much explosive to use. Or more likely, Bolan decided, whoever had actually placed the explosive wanted the dead man blamed but didn't want the structure destroyed.

Bolan looked at Sonda Mgabe. All of the fury was gone, and she suddenly looked exhausted.

Bolan asked a pointed question. "Do you think he set off the explosives?"

Sonda shook her head and smiled sadly. "Kenny? Not if his life depended on it. He believed in reconciliation, not combat." She laughed bitterly. "I'm more likely to have done it than Kenny."

"Then it's a setup," he stated bluntly. "Any idea who's behind the bombing?"

She nodded, jerking a thumb at the bodies of the three thugs. "These men used to work for him as enforcers, like the Mafia in your country."

"Who?"

"The functional head of the Bureau of State Security in the Transvaal. Major Pieter Volksmann."

"Got proof?"

Her voice was filled with cold anger. "I don't need any. Kenny's death is proof enough."

"I'd like to find your brother's evidence anyway. It might help expose the people who make it possible for someone like this Major Volksmann to stay in business. Do you know where he might have hid it?"

She shook her head. "I didn't know he had stuck his neck out and gathered such proof. It was so unlike him."

Bolan glanced at the bodies. "These three were looking for his papers, too." He pointed to the Beretta 93-R in her left hand. "If you're done with it."

Reluctantly she handed it back.

"Go back to the United States. We don't need your help. This is our war, and we can win it by ourselves."

He heard the pride in her voice.

"If you don't have a professional snake handler among you," he reminded her, "and you've got a nest of vipers, get yourself someone who knows how to get rid of them."

"You're a reporter. What do you know about fighting the bigots in our country?"

"I've been fighting people like them for a long time," Bolan replied, "and I'm still among the living."

He saw the indecision in her face. "We've got a little time before they send somebody to see what's holding up these three. Let's see if we can find your brother's papers."

She hesitated for a moment, then finally nodded in agreement.

Together they searched through the chaos the dead trio had created.

THE PRESS CONFERENCE outside the Voortrekker Monument had gone well. Reporters and television crews from at least twenty countries had attended. And when Major Volksmann took them down the corridor to where the explosion had occurred, they reacted exactly as he had expected.

Back in his office, Volksmann's main concern was for the three men he had sent to search Mgabe's flat. Whether they had found any documents in the man's home or not, they should have called in by now.

The major lifted his telephone and pushed a button. "Get Vanderwoerk and Majucs in here," he ordered.

Two heavyweights entered his office. Volksmann scribbled an address on a sheet of paper and handed it to Vanderwoerk.

"See what happened to the three men I sent to the kaffir's place to pick up the American reporter."

The pair of hardmen left, closing the door to Volksmann's office behind them.

He waited for a moment, then picked up his telephone and accessed a line that bypassed the switchboard. Dialing a number, he waited for someone to answer.

An English-accented voice on the other end of the line spoke. "Yes?"

"Volksmann here. Did you watch the news on television?"

"Not yet. I'll see it on the late news."

The major hesitated, then added, "You will make a deposit to my account in Zurich?"

There was a mild chuckle on the other end. "As soon as I finish watching the news, I'll authorize a transfer of funds."

A moment of silence passed. Then the voice added, "If there's nothing else you want to discuss..."

"No, no," Volksmann replied quickly.

Dropping the receiver onto its cradle, the major leaned back in his leather-covered swivel chair and closed his eyes.

He would soon have enough money on deposit to be able to vanish from South Africa before anybody examined his activities too closely. He'd choose someplace far away from the violence that had been part of his life for so many years.

Perhaps he'd even find a woman worthy of him. He wondered how he'd like a city like Buenos Aires.

THE THIN, GRAY-HAIRED black man was treating a patient when the phone rang. The semiconscious teenage boy on the examination table had been wounded in a street dispute with other black youths.

"Dr. Methabane," the elderly man answered.

"The Bureau of State Security arrested Kenneth Mgabe several hours ago and took him to King George Street. They charged him with terrorism," the voice on the other end reported. "A squad of undercover police is searching his apartment for evidence."

"Thank you for calling," Dr. Methabane replied politely. "What happened to the American reporter?"

"Volksmann's men are waiting for him to arrive. They plan to take him to King George Street, too."

"Call me if you find out anything else," the doctor said, and replaced the receiver.

He knew the caller would. As a porter in the central police station in central Pretoria, he could overhear confidential conversations without being noticed.

It was sad about Kenneth Mgabe, the doctor thought. The young man had been like a son to him. But then he'd turned away from his heritage to support a non-Zulu. He deserved whatever he got, even if he was Sonda's brother.

It was only with great reluctance that the doctor had asked one of his contacts to tell the security police about Kenny's meeting with the white American reporter. Harry Desmond had agreed to take credit for the information. It wouldn't look good if it was discovered that the head of the Zulu Action Front had been responsible for the arrest of another black man.

Taking the American reporter to the King George facility meant that BOSS didn't plan to let him live. Only those who disappeared forever were questioned there.

It would be a good thing if the American was found beaten and dead and BOSS was blamed. It would be another nail in the coffin of the whites.

What South Africa needed wasn't the reconciliation the new president preached, but action, and somebody who was willing to stand up and kill for his beliefs.

A name kept running through his thoughts, someone who could and would do that. His own. He didn't think he could get support if he ran. He hadn't discussed it with anyone yet, but he knew he could have become the power behind the new president if the Zulu candidate had won the election.

His dream could still come true—if the new president was assassinated and the citizens demanded a new election, instead of elevating one of the two vice-presidents.

He returned to the examination table. The young boy was still semiconscious. Dr. Methabane concentrated on trying to save his life.

BOLAN AND SONDA had searched every possible hiding place. None of the evidence turned up.

"The evidence isn't in this apartment," Bolan stated.

Sonda slumped into a small chair. "I could put together a list of many of the big shots backing the terrorists, but I suppose you can't publish it without proof."

"It would be a start," Bolan responded. "Much easier if we had hard evidence. But since we don't—"

The sound of a car screeching to a stop just outside the apartment interrupted his words. Carefully, he pulled aside the lowered shade and looked down into the road.

"I think we've got company."

Sonda got up and moved to his side. She stared out the living-room window at the two heavyset thugs who got out of a dark, official-looking car.

"State security police—" she looked at the three corpses Bolan had covered with sheets and blankets "—come to look for their mates."

"I thought so," Bolan agreed. "They were either that or enforcers from some local gang."

Sonda shook her head. "I'm not sure. All I am sure of is that they weren't invited to come here by my brother."

Bolan checked the clip in his Beretta. It was half-empty. He reached into a side pocket and replaced it.

Sonda copied his example and checked the clip in her H&K. It was full.

Bolan looked at her. "Sure you know how to use that?"

"As well as you. Where Kenny and I were raised, you had a choice of defending yourself or becoming a statistic of the violence that plagues this nation." She pushed her jaw forward arrogantly. "I'm still here."

Bolan liked her spunk and toughness. She hadn't turned pale and collapsed when she saw the three bodies. He was glad that for the moment they were on the same side. But for how long?

4

Bolan decided to take the confrontation outside where there was more room to maneuver. Sonda followed him out to the landing, her H&K firmly seated in her right hand.

The Executioner had switched weapons. He returned his 9 mm Beretta 93-R to the shoulder holster and substituted the .44 Magnum Desert Eagle. He'd need all the stopping power of the Israeli-made weapon, in case the two hardmen moving toward them were wearing bulletproof vests.

Carrying a 240-grain load, the large autopistol pumped lead at a velocity of 1537 foot-seconds. Even wearing chest protectors, people didn't stand a chance against its impact.

The two gaudily clad street soldiers moved up the steps, then saw Bolan looking down at them.

"That's far enough," he snapped.

"It is against the law to carry a weapon without a permit," the nearer man announced stiffly, looking at the large weapon in Bolan's right hand.

"No problem. Come and get it."

The hardman turned to his companion and nodded. Then he faced Bolan and slipped a hand under his jacket.

The muzzle of an Ingram MAC-10 submachine gun sprung into view. The security cop wrapped his finger around the trigger.

Bolan knew the weapon was capable of emptying a 30-round magazine in seconds. He didn't waste time or words. Snapping off a shot at the heavyset enforcer, the Executioner twisted out of the way of the screaming stream of 9 mm parabellum slugs that scarred the area where he'd been standing.

Bolan's bullet had drilled into the hardman's mouth, shattering his teeth and exiting the back of his head in a spray of blood and gore. Only the bulk of his partner standing behind prevented him from falling down the stairs.

The second hardman shoved the corpse away as he aimed at Bolan's chest. There was no time for the Executioner to get out of the way of the rounds the SIG-Sauer P-226 was about to spit at him.

A trio of explosions erupted behind Bolan. He didn't waste time turning his head. He knew that Sonda Mgabe had fired her H&K.

The street tough looked up at Bolan, his glazed eyes reflecting his uncertainty about who had killed him, then he fell on top of his dead partner.

Bolan moved back but kept his weapon pointed at the two bodies. Kicking the weapons away from the two still forms, he knelt and checked for pulses in their necks.

Satisfied they were dead, he stood and turned to Sonda. "You do know how to handle a gun."

There was a matter-of-fact quality in her voice as she replied, "They deserved to die. They had come to kill us." She glanced at the weapon in Bolan's hand. "Where did you learn to handle a gun so well?"

"Vietnam." It was a convenient explanation and true. "In my country killers don't put their guns away because you wave a press pass."

"The world has become a dangerous place."

He glanced at the bodies, then turned back to her. "BOSS agents?"

"If they were," she answered, "they weren't planning to tell us."

"Whoever sent them will come after you next," Bolan warned.

"Nobody knew I was here."

"The woman who called you about your brother knows."

"She won't talk. She hates BOSS as much I do."

"Let's get out of here before somebody else shows up."

She nodded. "Anyway, I didn't bring any spare magazines."

Bolan understood her. Like himself, the young woman apparently had a simple philosophy. It was the same one that had kept him alive for so many years: keep your weapons loaded and kill your enemy before he kills you.

"About that list..." he started to say.

"I'll need some time to put it together," she replied. "Call me in a few days."

The warrior wasn't sure there was time, but he said nothing to discourage her.

She reached into her shoulder bag and took out a card case and a pen. Handing Bolan a business card, she said, "My office number is on the front." She scribbled something on the back of the card. "That's my home number. I might be hard to reach. I do a lot of traveling and night work."

Bolan studied the card she handed him.

"I knew you were with the government." There was no title under her name. "What do you do for them?"

"I'm one of the people responsible for the personal safety of the president and his family. In your country you'd call me a bodyguard."

Bolan whistled. He'd been on target with his initial assessment of her. There was an experienced killing machine behind the attractive face and seductive figure.

She poised her pen against the blank back of a business card. "How do I reach you?"

"I've got a lot of places to go and people to see. But I'll keep in touch," he promised.

He had things to do that he could do better alone. He didn't mind putting his life on the block, but there was no point putting hers there, too, until it was absolutely necessary.

5

Located a short distance north of Johannesburg, the large mansion inside the walled estate was a perfect example of Tudor architecture. Even the armed guards that patrolled the perimeters day and night didn't detract from its unique elegance.

The showpiece of the home was the massive living room, furnished with rare antiques from around the world. A priceless painting by El Greco hung next to an early Picasso, from the period before he explored abstract symbolism.

A huge Persian rug that cost as much as a small private jet covered a small part of the enormous inlaid wooden floor and was the platform for a conversation area tastefully filled with furniture from the Queen Anne period.

On the wall behind the seated small, balding man were portraits of his grandparents and parents, painted by some of the finest European artists.

Harry Desmond's ancestors were soldiers who helped wrest the South African provinces from the Dutch in the early 1800s, then stayed to see what treasures they could find.

One of the treasures was the elegant desk that sat at one end of the room. The great Theophilus Shepstone, who had been appointed the first chief native commissioner by the British prime minister, had once ruled South Africa from that desk.

The elderly man shed the dark scarlet smoking jacket he'd been wearing, revealing the silk shirt underneath, and studied the faces in the portraits. Thanks to their fortitude in grabbing diamond-mining claims near Kimberley and gold claims on the Witwatersrand, he was one of the wealthiest men in South Africa.

It was his intention to retain his holdings and his fortune at any cost: donations to the various political movements, bribes to government officials, even the hiring of professionals to eliminate anyone who might be a threat.

He thought of something. Pushing the small red button that was mounted under the desk, he waited for someone to respond.

The door opened. A huge man in his late thirties entered, buttoning the jacket of his dark suit.

"Something you wanted, sir?"

Desmond smiled. The man was not only his personal secretary, but also chief of the cadre of men who guarded the estate.

"Yes, Arthur," he replied. "There may be a transfer to Major Volksmann's bank account."

"How much?"

"Twenty thousand rand. But wait until after the late news program."

The light blond man made a face. Desmond knew he had no respect for officials who accepted bribes.

"This isn't like the Special Action Forces, Arthur. We have to learn to work with anybody, even people like Major Volksmann, if we want to survive."

"Yes, sir." The flatness in the other man's voice communicated his understanding but no acceptance of the reality.

Desmond glanced at the bulge in the other man's jacket and knew it was caused by a weapon worn in shoulder harness. It was probably the American-manufactured .45 ACP Colt Gold Cup National Match he had purchased for him.

"I've told you before, Arthur. I won't have you wearing weapons inside the house."

"Yes, sir," the man replied softly. "I forgot to take it off."

"Do check on the guards before you retire."

The dark-suited bodyguard nodded.

As he turned to leave, a white-coated elderly black man entered, carrying a silver tray that bore a bottle of rare brandy and a crystal snifter.

The servant set the tray on a nearby wooden table and started to leave.

"Thank you, Emmanuel. I don't know what I would do if you weren't here to take care of me," he added in a patronizing tone.

Smiling, the man left the mammoth room while the mining magnate filled the snifter with brandy.

Desmond let his mind wander back to the political situation. The new president had to go. Alive or dead. He had nothing against him personally. After all, his own ancestors went to war to give everyone in the Cape settlement equal rights. This was strictly business.

But having blacks take over the government meant he had to start developing a completely new list of government officials to bribe. That was a young man's work. It had taken him almost half a lifetime to build the right contacts in the previous governments. He was getting too old to find people in the new administration willing to trade favors for money.

For a price he was certain Pieter Volksmann would be able to find someone from one of the right-wing groups he supported to turn the president into a martyr.

Killing the head of state made good business sense. But it had to be a black who killed him, he decided. Otherwise, discontented black miners, resentful that a white man had murdered their icon, could slow down or stop production in his mines.

The most logical choice would be for a Zulu to do the killing. Their leaders were always claiming that they had a right to rule South Africa because they were the country's largest tribe. Perhaps he could convince the Zulu activists that letting a black who wasn't one of their own run the country was as bad as letting the right-wing whites stay in power.

How to get the message to them? Dr. Methabane? They had done business before. All Methabane ever talked about was the right of the Zulus to rule South Africa and the group's constant need for additional funds. The head of the Zulu Action Front might be receptive—if there was enough money in it for him.

Of course, if it became necessary, he'd have to come up with someone who wasn't a Zulu to eliminate the new president. Perhaps Arthur would have a suggestion.

The former military officer knew a lot of people, both in South Africa and the surrounding countries. He was certain that despite Arthur's aversion to blacks, the man knew at least one of them who was a professional.

It was comforting to have someone like Arthur working for him.

AROUND THE CORNER from the large hospital, Bolan sat behind the wheel of the Audi 500 and thought about what the enforcer from the security police had muttered before he died.

They had to have known he was coming to meet with Kenneth Mgabe. But how?

Only Brognola, Mgabe and he knew.

Somebody Mgabe told about the meeting? Someone he trusted? Like his sister? It didn't seem likely. She looked genuinely shocked when she heard he was killed.

Something was going on that he didn't understand. At least not yet. If Mgabe didn't plant the explosives, someone else did.

Volksmann?

According to the news bulletin, the Bureau of State Security had shown up right after the explosion. At least Major Pieter Volksmann had.

It smelled like a setup, but he needed proof.

After some telephone calls to several newspapers, Bolan learned that dead criminals were usually taken to the morgue in the HP Verwoerd Hospital on Belvedere, right in Pretoria. He'd decided that it was time to take a personal look at the young man the police had labeled a terrorist.

He locked the doors of the rental car and walked to the main door of the large medical center. He checked his wristwatch. The glowing hands stood out in the darkness. It was close to 1:00 a.m.

Bolan looked through the large glass doors. The main lobby was nearly empty, except for a security guard.

Wearing a combat blacksuit and camouflage makeup, Bolan waited in a dark corner. He had his hand on the Beretta 93-R, which was seated in the shoulder rig. The Desert Eagle pressed against the small of his back.

The guard yawned as he peered down the main corridor, then walked around the corner.

The Executioner slipped through the glass doors and checked the directory board. The morgue was in the basement.

Taking a nearby flight of stairs two at a time, he reached the basement level, then opened the door just enough to check the corridor.

Empty.

He slid against the wall, stopping at a cork bulletin board. He glanced at it. Someone had posted a poorly photocopied notice that one of the terrorist groups—the Order of Death—would be sponsoring an antigovernment rally that weekend for whites only.

Bolan ripped the announcement from the board and slipped it into a pocket. Then he continued his movement until he reached the door to the morgue.

Gripping the Beretta firmly, he opened the door.

The room was dark. Bolan found a series of light switches and turned them on.

The room itself looked and felt like a giant refrigerator. Rows of horizontal stainless-steel doors lined three of the walls, each door bearing a stamped number.

Pushed against one of the walls were two stainless-steel examination tables. A small metal desk and chair stood next to them.

The familiar pungent aroma of formaldehyde permeated the area. Bolan had been in too many rooms like this not to recognize the chemical that covered the smell of death.

He searched through the papers on the desk for a list that specified whose body was behind each door. Nothing.

There was a computerized list of human inventory in the top center drawer. Running his finger down the corpse inventory, he couldn't find Kenneth Mgabe's name.

Had somebody already claimed the body? He didn't think so.

Bolan heard the door begin to open. He moved to the light switches and darkened the room, then pressed himself against the wall, feeling the weight of the Beretta in his hand.

A small man with thinning brown hair pushed the door open and entered the morgue. Automatically the doctor's hand found the switches and turned them on. The white coat he wore had his name sewn on an upper-right pocket: Dr. Ferdi Orande.

He was too busy studying the contents of the folder in his hands to notice the opened desk drawer.

Bolan stepped into the light.

"Dr. Orande, are you the chief pathologist?"

Orande was startled by the blacksuited apparition in front of him. He stared, wide-eyed, at the Beretta.

"*Ja,*" he answered nervously in an Afrikaans accent.

"Where is Kenneth Mgabe's body?"

The doctor froze. "I don't recognize that name."

"The black terrorist the police brought in. Where is he?"

The doctor started to say something, then stared at the weapon in Bolan's hand and pointed a quivering finger at one of the walls with doors.

"Thirty-two."

Bolan prodded the doctor with the Beretta to lead the way.

"Open it," he ordered.

"The police told me that..." The pathologist looked at the cold expression on Bolan's face and stopped talking. He pulled open the door.

Bolan slid the tray out, revealing a body covered with a plastic sheet. "Bring one of those examination carts over."

He watched as Orande rushed to follow his orders.

"Help me get him on the table," the big American demanded. Together they lowered the body to the mobile examination table.

Bolan studied the body. The chest and stomach had been torn open. He looked at the doctor. "What killed him? The explosion?"

The doctor began to shake. "You'll have to ask the police."

"Did you conduct the autopsy, Doctor?"

"I'm not supposed to talk about—"

"You did write a report."

Words spilled from Orande's mouth. "I am under official orders not to—"

"The report, Doctor," Bolan insisted. "Where is it?"

The pathologist sneaked a glance at a small, locked file cabinet.

"Please ask the Bureau of State Security for a copy," he pleaded.

"I'm asking *you.*"

He pushed the nervous man toward the file cabinet.

"Please don't kill me."

The doctor began to perspire, despite the chill of the morgue. His shaking hands retrieved keys from a coat pocket. With difficulty he fit the key into the file-cabinet lock and opened it.

"Save me time and get it for me," Bolan ordered.

Quickly the pathologist pulled out a folder and handed it to the Executioner, who studied the report. The doctor had found five 9 mm slugs lodged in vital organs.

Smiling coldly, he forced the small man to lead the way out of the morgue and up the stairs to the main lobby.

"Stop," Bolan ordered, as he saw the security guard walking by. The uniformed hospital cop waited in front of an elevator and, when the doors opened, he boarded it.

The pair walked through the main doors. "Wait fifteen minutes before you call anybody," Bolan said, then added, "I can always come back."

As he vanished into the shadows, Bolan knew he was about to make Major Pieter Volksmann's life hell.

6

Bolan drove to Johannesburg and found a twenty-four-hour photocopy shop. He moved to a self-service machine and started running off copies of the autopsy report.

According to the telephone book, he'd need twenty-nine copies for the major news outlets. And Brognola would need one.

He'd planned something else for this night, but what he was doing seemed important. And the arms depot wasn't going anywhere.

The process took the better part of two hours, including stapling sets of the report. The shop also sold plain large envelopes. Bolan ordered thirty and paid the bill.

Sitting in the rented car, he stuffed a report in each envelope.

Making the rounds of the newspaper and television bureau offices took another two hours. For the most part, there was no receptionist, so he handed the envelope to the first person he encountered and asked that it be given to whoever was in charge of news.

AT THE WORLD NEWS bureau offices, the weary news editor pushed her glasses into her hair and rubbed her eyes. It had been a long day, covering the violence that accompanied the new president as he went through the country, meeting with different ethnic groups. The various terrorist gangs tried to disrupt his appearances, often clashing with each other, sometimes armed with guns and knives.

To Irene Wexler the situation seemed like a Loony Tunes cartoon. The terrorist groups acted as though they refused to believe that a black man could be president of South Africa, and were determined to prove it, even if they had to try to kill him.

Only the intervention of volunteer guards and the number of policemen willing to stand up to them had stopped them so far.

Although the Johannesburg bureau had been open only since February, the amount of news coming out of South Africa was already overwhelming. Irene Wexler had begged the network's stateside headquarters to send more camera crews. The three they had assigned her weren't enough to cover all of the incidents.

One of the late-shift news writers walked past her desk and dropped a manila envelope in front of her.

Irene looked up. "What's this, Charley?"

"Don't know. Some huge hunk of a guy said to give it to you."

"What guy? Who was he?"

"You wouldn't forget him if you saw him. Coldest eyes I've ever seen." He thought for a moment. "He sounded like an American."

Wexler looked puzzled as she tore open the envelope. Her expression changed from curious to suspicious to excited as she glanced through the enclosed documents.

She looked up at Charley, her eyes wider than the writer had ever seen before, and handed him the photocopied pages. The long whistle came involuntarily as he read the pages.

He looked at her. "Think this is legit?"

She was about to answer when her phone rang.

"Wexler," she said into the receiver. After a pause she continued, "No, I didn't hear about that.... Yeah, we pay for real news tips. Let me check it out and I'll get back to you. Give me your name, address and telephone number."

She scribbled some information on the top sheet of a ruled pad, then hung up.

Looking at the rewrite man, she smiled. "I think we've got a live one. A few hours ago some huge guy forced the pathologist at Verwoerd Hospital to give him the autopsy report of Kenneth Mgabe."

"What do we do with it?"

"You get something on paper for Judy Thompson's morning news program while I make some calls to get comments."

The news writer picked up the pages and ran full speed to his desk. This one, he knew, would be played on every affiliate around the world.

Similar reactions were taking place at every office where Bolan had dropped copies of the report. Nobody wanted to take the chance that the competition would beat them. Not with the impact the story would have on the public.

CALLS FROM MEMBERS of the news media jammed the telephone lines at the central police station in Pretoria.

Pieter Volksmann forced himself to sound pleasant and official to each of the callers, promising to investigate and call them back. But the questions they asked strongly implied that he was lying or covering up information.

They wouldn't have dared make such accusations in the old days. The members of the press once knew their place. They used to exist simply to disseminate official information.

The few who had tried to defy the government were shut down because they violated the censorship rules. Those newspapers that managed to stay open and publish antigovernment lies found that their advertisers canceled their contracts. If that didn't work, their presses were destroyed.

It was different now. The government had decided to coddle the reporters and television newspeople who were accusing the security bureau of harassing citizens. Some went as far as accusing it of murder.

He was tempted to call the national head of the Bureau of State Security and ask for his advice, but decided against it. He knew what he would be told: *If you can't handle the press, I'll put someone in your place who can.*

The risk was too great. What if his replacement started checking and found out about the gifts he had received for doing favors?

No, he'd have to take care of it himself.

The problem was he didn't know where to start. He had a sketch of what the American looked like—at least as far as the clerk at the airport car-rental counter could remember—but he couldn't issue a Wanted poster without bringing unwanted attention to BOSS.

He'd have to wait until the man who called himself Belasko made a move. Then he could unleash the full power of the bureau against him.

ONLY AN OCCASIONAL gunshot punctuated the Soweto evening. It was a relatively quiet night for the huge black township.

Inside the small infirmary, Dr. Methabane asked a question. "Who is Mike Belasko?" He sat on a stool in the examination room and waited for the young woman to answer.

"He claims to be an American reporter," Sonda Mgabe replied, holding a lit cigarette between her fingers.

"He is a white. Therefore, he cannot be believed," the leader of the Zulu Action Front stated. "Find out who he really represents."

"And if he is who he claims to be?"

"Perhaps we can use him to avenge the murder of your brother."

Sonda took a puff from the cigarette and nodded. As usual, Dr. Methabane had come up with a reasonable suggestion.

NONE OF THE UPROAR he'd created seemed to bother Bolan. He was bushed from lack of sleep, and there was still one more thing he had to do before he could think of resting.

He pulled into an all-night truck stop and ordered a large container of coffee to go. His next appointment required he be alert and fast.

One of the men sitting at the counter turned to him. From the unshaven man's attire, Bolan assumed he was a trucker.

The man had a heavy Afrikaans accent. "You hear about that crazy kaffir who tried to blow up the Voortrekker Monument?"

Bolan shook his head. It was late, and he had too much to do to get in a pointless argument.

"Give them buggers an inch and they'll steal your house. We got to stick together and make sure they don't take over our country."

He waited for Bolan to comment, but the big American remained silent.

The man reached into his pocket and pulled out a folded piece of paper.

"You signed up with any group yet?"

"Group?"

"You know, make these kaffirs know who's still boss." He opened the folded paper and handed it to the Executioner.

"This is a good one. Not like those cuckoo heads in the AWB and the White Wolves. Just a bunch of decent Christian men trying to protect their homes and their families from those black savages."

Bolan glanced at the paper. It announced a recruiting meeting for one of the terrorist gangs, the White Security Guard, Friday night at a tavern on the edge of Pretoria.

The waitress handed Bolan the container of coffee. He paid and turned to leave.

"Show up," the unshaven man said. "You look like the kind of man we need."

Bolan pocketed the announcement. He had a better use for it.

7

The sign over the steel doors of the small building stated the warehouse belonged to the South African Information Distribution Company, Ltd. But according to the information Brognola had passed along to Bolan, the building's real function was the storage of weapons and ammunition for the White Wolves.

Bolan had searched through the factory district of Johannesburg until three in the morning before he located the brick structure. He drove slowly around the building, looking for possible entrances and exits, then searched for a secluded place to park the Audi.

Several semitrailers sat on a side street. He pulled behind one of them and parked.

As he sipped the hot coffee, he mulled over what he knew about the group and their weapons depot.

Bolan had gone up against the White Wolves before, and they had a reputation for conducting raids on black-township families, bombing community centers and churches and for the random killing of blacks.

The weapons inventory inside the building, according to Brognola's sources, was substantial. It took money to acquire that many guns, rifles, explosives, armored vehicles and ammunition.

Bolan finished drinking his coffee and shoved the empty paper cup under the car seat. He reached down for the canvas carryall on the floor next to him and opened it.

The warrior had no way of knowing if anyone was inside. The building could be empty, or a squad of terrorists could be camped in there. The only thing Bolan was sure of was that he had to be ready for anything.

From inside the bag he pulled out the shoulder rig for his Beretta 93-R. The handgun was lying next to it. He checked the clip, which was full. The gun slid easily into the holster.

The Israeli hand cannon was next. Checking the clip, he made sure the .44-caliber Desert Eagle's magazine was full. Then he pushed the handgun into the holster already mounted at the back of his belt.

A pair of 9 mm Uzi machine pistols stared up at him, and Bolan debated whether he should carry one of them. He checked the load of one of the Uzis, then slid the weapon's sling onto his left shoulder.

His mission was to destroy the arms cache inside, and the plastic explosives in the carryall should accomplish that. There was a thin nylon rucksack shoved in a corner of the carryall that would make carrying the C-4 easier, and leave his hands free to use his weapons if he ran into opposition.

Five C-4 packets, already fitted with detonators and timers, were carefully lowered into the nylon backpack. Bolan slipped the bag on his back and worked his way around the building to a small loading platform.

He had noticed a glass-paned door to the right of the dock, and he gently turned the handle. The door was locked, as he expected it would be.

He had remembered to bring a small glass cutter and a roll of sticky tape. Carefully he scored the glass pane nearest the door handle, tapped the cut edges and separated the glass from the frame, then used several lengths of the sticky tape he had attached to the pane to pull it out.

Reaching through the small opening, he felt around. There was only a door-handle lock. Surprised at the lack of security, Bolan could only assume that the warehouse was full of armed guards.

Easing the door open, he slipped inside. He let his eyes get used to the darkness, then went to search for possible live opposition.

THE TWO MEN in sweat-stained light brown uniforms sat around the small table in the office. A double deck of cards was in front of one of them, weapons nearby on the floor.

The short, slender man in his fifties smiled at the other middle-aged man and started to shuffle the cards.

"How about another game of blackjack?"

"You've been on this gambling thing ever since you got back from Sun City, Mies," his companion commented.

Sun City was a major gambling resort—a miniature Las Vegas—located two hours north of Johannesburg by car. It was one of the major sources of revenue for the Bophuthatswana Homeland.

"Talk is cheap, Josef," Mies replied. "Put your money where your mouth is, as the Americans say."

"I think you went there to sleep with a kaffir woman. Come on, confess. How was she?" Josef asked.

Mies was getting annoyed. "Do you want to play? Yes or no."

Josef sighed. The game had already cost him fifty rand. "Let's wait until Hendrik and Karl get back from doing their rounds."

Looking disappointed, Mies put down the cards. "I guess I should see if they need any help. Josef, you wait here in case the commandant calls."

Mies grabbed the weapon sitting on the floor, a 9 mm Cobray M-11 submachine gun, manufactured in the United States. The SMG was noted for its ability to discharge a 30-round magazine in less than six seconds. Only the steadiest hand could keep the weapon focused on its target once its rounds were released.

"If a sexy-sounding woman calls," Mies said over his shoulder as he headed out the door, "invite her over. I'm ready for her."

The sentry at the table looked disgusted. "Is that all you think of, women and gambling? You need a wife, Mies."

Mies didn't hear the remark. He had already vanished into the warehouse area.

BOLAN MOVED SILENTLY through the warehouse. High wooden shelves lined one wall and were filled with stacks of books and pamphlets. Bolan picked up one: *The Worldwide Jew Conspiracy*.

He dropped the book back on the pile and studied the titles of several others. Each was a duplication of Nazi literature, translated into Afrikaans. The shelves were filled with hate literature.

He wondered if anyone still believed the transparent lies printed in the inventoried material. Probably, he decided, or there would be no point in publishing them.

From what he'd been told, the White Wolves operated a number of hate-literature shops throughout South Africa.

As he glanced at the rows of bound literature, he realized he could do more than just destroy an arms cache. He could also demolish a major source of hate information.

He took out one of the plastic-explosive packets and set the timer. He had thirty-five minutes to finish up and get out.

As he moved down a wide aisle between two rows of wooden shelves, Bolan heard footsteps. He sprinted to the end of the aisle and pressed himself against a wall, hiding in the shadows the book stacks had created.

He eased the Uzi from his shoulder and waited for the individual to appear.

Bolan lowered the weapon and gripped it tightly as he heard the footsteps coming closer, then stop.

Bolan readied himself as a vague shadow appeared on the floor in front of him.

The shadow was holding a Heckler & Koch MP-5 SMG.

Bolan pushed the Uzi at him.

The man snarled and brought up his weapon. Anticipating the move, Bolan spun out of the way. The shooter tried to follow his target's movement, but he was having trouble keeping the MP-5 from shooting its rounds into the ceiling.

Bolan triggered a triburst, the first round puncturing Karl's sternum and shoving the man back into a stack of books. The second and third punched holes in his stomach. The shooter dropped his weapon and crumpled to the floor.

Bolan turned to retrieve his rucksack when he felt a blow across his shoulders. Staggering from the unexpected attack, he lost his balance and fell against the wooden shelving. The Uzi fell from his hands.

Still stunned, he turned and saw a slender man slashing down at him with the metal buttstock of a submachine gun. He rolled away just in time to avoid a second blow.

The attacker quickly reversed the weapon in his hand and rammed his finger in front of the trigger.

Bolan kicked upward between his assailant's legs, smashing his booted toe into the man's genitals. Grunting with pain, the slender man staggered backward, but managed to hold on to his weapon.

The Executioner knew there was no time to retrieve the Uzi. He released the Ka-bar blade from its forearm sheath as he rolled sideways again.

The guard, still grimacing from the pain of his adversary's kick, pulled back on the trigger. The weapon jammed.

Bolan took advantage of his lucky break and wrapped his hands around a wooden upright. He could feel the pain of the bruised shoulder as he pulled himself to his feet.

Jumping at the man, Bolan wrapped an arm around his neck and pulled the razor sharp Ka-bar knife across his attacker's carotid artery.

Red blood spurted from the severed vessel, soaking the man's uniform shirt and spattering on Bolan's hand. Releasing the guard, the Executioner watched him sag into the wooden shelves, then slide down to the ground.

He wiped his bloodied hand with a rag he found nearby, picked up the fallen Uzi and checked his watch.

Taking out the two men had taken fifteen minutes. Only twenty minutes remained on the timer.

He moved back to where he had left the rucksack.

As he knelt, a sound alerted Bolan and he whirled. A large man started to fire the 9 mm Cobray subgun in his massive hands.

Only Bolan's quick reaction saved him. Dropping the Uzi, he threw himself toward the shooter as soon he heard the metallic click of a trigger moving. The rounds chewed into the concrete floor behind him, kicking miniclouds of dust into the air.

Bolan yanked the Desert Eagle from its holster and fired twice. Both rounds ripped into the fat man's right side, missing vital organs, and made him stumble.

Bellowing in rage, the shooter aimed his subgun at Bolan's head. Before he could pull back on the heavy trigger, the Executioner corrected his aim and fired two slugs into the enraged man's chest.

Bits of shattered breastbone and tissue flew from the newly opened crater, and blood gushed from the gaping wound as the gunner fell to the floor.

The Executioner retrieved the Uzi and slung it over a shoulder, then he dropped the clip on the Desert Eagle. As he snapped a fresh clip in and pulled himself to his feet, Bolan sensed rather than heard movement behind him.

Raising the Desert Eagle as he turned, Bolan drew a bead on the hardman's chest before his adversary could level his SMG. The big .44 bucked, and the man's chest opened up in a spray of blood, then he collapsed to the floor, his SMG clattering beside him.

Ignoring the pain in his bruised shoulder, Bolan picked up his rucksack, moved quietly down the wide aisle and made his way to the small door ahead.

He stood to one side, braced himself, then swung around and kicked open the door. His .44 Magnum up and probing, Bolan made a quick survey of the area.

The room was unoccupied. Only a double deck of cards and an ashtray filled with cigarette butts indicated that anybody had been in there.

The former occupants were dead. All of them, he hoped.

A second door led from the room. Bolan opened it carefully and listened. Nothing.

Working his way around the door and along the adjacent wall, he steadied his weapon, ready to take on anyone who might be there.

All around him, stacked to the ceiling, were crates, mostly sealed. Their markings indicated they had originated in many countries—boxes from the United States, China, Spain, Argentina, Switzerland and Belgium. All of them were filled with handguns, rifles, grenades, missiles and launchers and ammunition.

He moved up and down the aisles, alert for hidden attackers. Finally satisfied he was alone, Bolan started to plant the rest of the plastique and set the timers.

Finally done, he checked his wristwatch. He had fifteen minutes left to decide if he needed to replenish his own inventory.

Feeling the bone-deep pain in his shoulder, he thought of leaving without forcing his injured shoulder to support the weight of additional supplies. Another dozen fragmentation grenades might come in handy, he decided as he changed his mind and packed them in the rucksack.

Several cases of 9 mm ammunition caught his attention. He grabbed a handful of boxes from an opened crate and packed them beside the grenades.

A stack of crates containing Heckler & Koch Model 94 carbines caused him to stop. He had fired the relatively compact weapon before and knew it could pump a lot of lead in seconds. He decided to take a pair with him in case his Uzi automatics became inoperable for some reason. Loading magazines and ammo for the carbines into the rucksack, he shouldered the weapons and lifted the unwieldy load.

He reached the car and dropped the shoulder bag next to the canvas carryall on the floor. Reaching into a pocket, he found the notice for the White Security Guard recruiting meeting. A rusty nail in a nearby wooden power pole made an excellent hanger.

Bolan got in the vehicle and fired the ignition. Then he looked back at the small building. He had accomplished two things tonight: exposed the lie about Kenneth Mgabe's death and destroyed the literature and weapons of hate.

As he drove away, he remembered something else he had accomplished. He had planted seeds of suspicion about who was responsible for the soon-to-be-demolished warehouse.

Loud thunder roared through the air as the plastic explosives released their destructive energy. Through his rearview mirror he could see flames shooting into the sky, consuming the large storage facility.

Fire trucks rushed past him, heading for the holocaust. He slowed to let them pass, then sped up again and drove in the opposite direction.

8

The gray sky was starting to give way to sunlight when Mack Bolan stopped at a run-down restaurant on the way back to Pretoria to order breakfast. He waited for the bleached blond waitress behind the counter to notice him, but she and her handful of customers were too busy watching a news program on television to pay attention to the newcomer. What enthralled them was a replay of the bombing of the Voortrekker Monument.

The newscaster added a new dimension to the story.

"Our staff has just obtained a copy of a confidential report from the chief pathologist at the HF Verwoerd Hospital, who examined the body of the slain speech writer, Kenneth Mgabe. The report indicates that the young black man had not been killed by the explosion at the Voortrekker Monument, but by five shots from a 9 mm gun.

"Since it is now obvious Mr. Mgabe didn't set the explosives, then who did? Is this another attempt by advocates of apartheid to discredit the new black president?

"This commentator hopes that the South African police will be as diligent in searching for the killer or killers of Kenneth Mgabe as they are in hunting for black terrorists."

The Executioner imagined the BOSS major would be seething as he watched the news.

He looked around the restaurant. The few customers and the waitress looked disgusted.

Turning to Bolan, the woman behind the counter shook her head. "The kaffirs have done enough bad things without this. BOSS didn't have to go and make them sound like angels by blaming them for something they didn't do."

She turned her head back to the television without asking Bolan if he wanted to order.

He gave up trying to get breakfast. As he got up from the counter stool, he wondered how the major would explain the autopsy report.

VOLKSMANN HAD CALLED an emergency meeting, and his office was crowded with men and women who looked annoyed at having been summoned from personal activities.

Some of them were still officially on the BOSS payroll, while others were being paid from secret contributions.

"As you might have heard, a warehouse on the edge of the city, filled with arms, was destroyed last night. We believe we know what group is responsible and are questioning them."

He had been awakened at dawn by a lengthy call from the head of the local branch of the White Wolves complaining about the loss of the arms depot.

"The damned White Security Guard did it!" the telephone voice shouted. "I have proof."

He demanded replacements if Volksmann expected them to continue their activities.

After making a few calls, the BOSS major was certain the press would never find out about the arms in the warehouse. Officially the explosion would be blamed on a leaky gas pipe.

There was something else he wanted to say to his people.

"The lies the newspaper and television reporters have been spreading about the death of the kaffir found at the monument have been an embarrassment to this department. The pathologist who prepared the false autopsy report has been arrested. When he was questioned this morning, he claimed that a man with an American accent forced him to write the lies.

"I believe that man was the American terrorist, Michael Belasko, who has already caused a great number of atrocities here. I also believe that kaffirs and their supporters hired him to start a private war against the white people of South Africa. He must be stopped!

"Five of our people are dead. Two days ago five loyal men were murdered, and we cannot find the murderer!"

He waited for somebody to speak. No one did.

"The American killed them. Let me tell you about this Belasko," Volksmann said, getting up and taking a seat on the edge of his desk. "I've made some inquiries."

The BOSS major had contacted Interpol, the FBI, the British secret service and Russian Intelligence. Only the Russians had anything on someone named Michael Belasko.

They faxed him their files.

Volksmann picked up the fax pages and read from them. "According to the Russians, Belasko was a former CIA agent who had gone private. He takes on assignments around the world whenever some government needs someone eliminated. They thought he had been killed in Iraq. Obviously he hadn't been.

"He is a trained assassin. An expert with weapons, martial arts and disguises. According to their files, he is a very large man. Two hundred pounds in weight and over six feet in height. With dark hair. They have no photographs of him.

"We have found someone who knows what he looks like. Each of you will receive copies of an artist's sketch of this terrorist before you leave the station. Show them around. Perhaps he is staying in a hotel. Check them for an American guest. Find him. Search every public place. If you see an American who even vaguely resembles his description, call for assistance." He slammed his hand on the desk. "But find him."

He dismissed them with a wave of his hand, then went behind his desk and fell back into the leather seat. When the last person left and closed the door behind him, Volksmann lifted the phone.

He knew how much Desmond hated getting calls, but this was too important to worry about arousing the mining magnate's displeasure.

Desmond answered on the third ring.

"Sorry to bother you, Mr. Desmond, but something has come up."

He told him about the destruction of the White Wolves' warehouse in the middle of the night.

"The head of the Pretoria chapter woke me up to tell me about it. They need replacements."

"What kind of weapons?"

"They asked for Heckler & Koch G-3 A-3 assault rifles—the ones that take 7.62 mm ammo—9 mm parabellum SIG-Sauer P-226s and a decent supply of ammunition for both." He paused, then added, "They said they could also use plastic explosives, timers, grenades and..." He hesitated. "One never knows what the opposition will come up with."

"I'm surprised they didn't ask you to get them some tanks and a nuclear device at the same time," Desmond said sarcastically.

Volksmann didn't reply. His contact would let himself be pushed just so far, and the major sensed the limits had been reached.

"I will go only so far," Desmond warned.

Volksmann understood. The man had said yes.

"Thank you," the major said. "After all, they are protecting our property. Without such organizations the kaffirs would steal everything."

There was a moment of silence, then the Englishman gave his answer. "Point heard and accepted. I'll have the suppliers contacted. They should have what the White Wolves want. You make the arrangements where the supplies should be delivered. I'll let you know when."

SONDA MGABE WAS ALSO in a meeting. The head of the Zulu Action Front had asked the elderly men who made up the inner council of the activist organization to get together and discuss several pressing issues. They were meeting in the small private home that was connected to his Soweto infirmary.

Ten old men and Sonda were seated around the wall in the living room. Standing behind them were two younger men, holding AK-47s.

"I am pleased that your brother has been vindicated," Dr. Abel Methabane told the young woman. "But that is not why we are here."

She nodded. Already a half-dozen friends had called to tell her the news. At least, she decided, Kenny would not be the scapegoat for accusations of black violence bandied about by the white hate groups.

What confused her was the identity of the person who had distributed copies of the autopsy report to the newspaper and television newspeople. No one had taken credit for doing that. At least not yet.

"My reason for calling you together is to discuss the political situation," Methabane said. "As you know, the press claims that the white terrorist groups are still trying to get rid of the new president. This concerns me, as it should every Zulu. I believe, as I'm sure you do, that a Zulu should have been elected president. But if the new head of state is assassinated, there is no one in his party popular enough to replace him." He paused to let the thought sink in.

"Only a Zulu could bring the blacks in South Africa together against the whites. Unfortunately, I called a senior official of the Inkatha Freedom Party, and he refused to discuss the possibility."

Sonda was incensed. "We are not employees of the Inkatha Party," she reminded Dr. Methabane.

"But we are Zulus," another member of the group stated.

"We are talking about politicians," she remarked sarcastically.

The elderly doctor smiled. Sonda had learned well. It was better she lectured the elderly council members than he. The leaders of the Zulu Action Party were tired of his preaching that they had the right to rule South Africa.

"So what do we do? The man who holds the office cannot hold the country together."

He didn't add that the new president wasn't the same man he had known twenty years earlier. That man had been a fiery revolutionary.

Age hadn't changed him. Twenty years in prison had. The man he used to know wouldn't compromise. It was bad enough that he wasn't a Zulu. It was worse that he was now sharing the rule of South Africa with the whites.

The doctor was about to speak again. He glanced at the window. Signaling the two armed men to his side, he leaned over and whispered something. Both men disappeared into the kitchen.

"Before suggestions are offered, let us take a brief recess," he said suddenly.

He nodded to Sonda, who stood and followed the lead of the two armed men.

OUTSIDE, A BLACK MAN in work clothes pressed a small eavesdropping device to the living-room window, trying to hear the conversation inside. His concentration was so great that he failed to hear the soft steps behind him.

The muzzle of a gun pressed into his neck.

"Turn very slow," a man's voice ordered, "with your hands above your head."

He did as he was ordered. Two armed men stared at him, the muzzles of their AK-47s aimed at the center of his chest.

"Why are you listening?"

The man tried to lie. "I wasn't listening. I was just trying to see if my friend William was home."

The explanation was rejected.

"Who sent you?"

"Nobody. I told you I was just looking for my—"

"If you have a wife and children, they will never see you again alive," one of the armed men warned. "Unless you speak the truth."

The eyes of the trapped man darted to the small Volkswagen parked at the grassy edge of the property. Another man, also black, was sitting behind the wheel.

The man in the car lowered the window.

Sonda, the doctor and other members of the council emerged from the house.

The man stared at her in shock.

"Sonda, why are you here?"

She recognized the man. Charley Lakuma. The man who sat in the car was another member of the government security staff, Mark Molefe, a former Soweto constable.

Dr. Methabane turned to the young woman. "You know these men?"

She nodded. "They are part of the government security force."

Turning to the captured eavesdropper, Methabane said, "Then you followed her here."

"No. We got a tip that the Zulu Front was having a secret meeting. We just wanted to make sure it had nothing to do with a plot against the president."

The man behind the wheel of the Volkswagen pushed the muzzle of an American-made MAC-10 submachine gun out of his opened window and aimed it at the elderly doctor.

Sonda grabbed the small H&K pistol from inside her purse and spun. A trio of slugs chugged into the face and neck of the driver. The MAC-10 SMG fell from his hands as his lifeless body collapsed over the top of the opened car window.

As blood gushed from the cavity in his face, Sonda turned quickly back to the other man.

In the sudden confusion, the eavesdropper wrested an AK-47 from one of the guards and turned it on the woman. Before he could pull the trigger, she emptied the rounds remaining in the pistol's clip into his chest.

Wearing stunned expressions, the council members stared at the two bodies. Only Dr. Methabane looked calm.

"Survival is the first rule when you live in a jungle like the one we find ourselves in today," he commented to the group.

Turning to Sonda, he added, "You acted wisely, child. To have done nothing would have destroyed all of us."

She didn't look convinced. "I knew the wife and children of the man at the window," she said softly, as if she were talking only to herself.

Then she walked away to where she had parked her small Japanese-made car.

The elderly doctor watched her leave, then turned to the council members. "If it becomes necessary," he promised them, "she will be the instrument through which this new president will be eliminated."

HARRY DESMOND WATCHED from the easy chair as Arthur came into the living room. "Did you reach the suppliers?"

"Just got off the telephone with them," the man replied in a clipped military tone.

"When will the shipment arrive?"

"Night after tomorrow. They'll fly everything in on helicopters. They said that wouldn't attract as much attention as a cargo jet."

Desmond ran his hand across his bald scalp as he thought. "Where will the pickup point be?"

"A small, private field in Mozambique, a few miles from the border."

"You've made the necessary arrangements to pay them?"

"All taken care of."

"Good. Be sure to contact Major Volksmann with the details."

Arthur nodded and left the room.

Desmond was pleased that someone with Arthur's many talents worked for him. It was almost impossible to get a good man these days.

9

Mack Bolan was tired, but there was still too much to do to give in to fatigue. It was morning, and he knew he was operating on pure adrenaline. None of that mattered at the moment. He had to contact Stony Man Farm. Brognola and his people would have access to information he needed.

The telephone in the subleased apartment wasn't secure. He had to find a pay phone from which he could place the overseas call.

He remembered a hotel at the corner of Paul Kruger and Scheiding. The Victoria Hotel. He knew he was taking a risk going out. The Bureau of State Security would have agents looking for a large American. But Bolan needed to make the overseas call and he was sure there would be a pay phone in the lobby of the hotel.

MAJOR VOLKSMANN HAD alerted his agents throughout the Transvaal in hope of sighting Mike Belasko. They had the police artist's sketch of what the American looked like.

Just outside the Victoria Hotel, a pair of BOSS field agents carefully studied the men going in and out of the old building. Most looked like what they were—diplomats from various countries with embassies in Pretoria.

The female of the pair saw a large man with the face of a prize fighter enter the lobby. Quickly she tugged at the sleeve of her male companion and pointed him out.

"That's Kurt Weitlandt. He's one of the top men with the White Wolves," he said in disgust, pulling her hand away.

"I never saw him before," she apologized.

"He's always dropping in to visit the major," the man said. "Use the sketch."

BOLAN WAS UNIMPRESSED with what he saw of Pretoria as he drove to the center of the small administrative capital. There were too many people—almost a million of them—too many foreign embassies, too many government offices and too many run-down monuments to the history of the country before its black citizens decided they also had rights.

To avoid unnecessary exposure, the Executioner parked his car behind the hotel and entered through a rear door. His passage took him through the dining-room kitchen.

Apologizing profusely, he said, "I must have come in through the wrong door."

Then, after studying the people in the lobby, he walked across to the three pay phones mounted on a far wall.

After getting the overseas operator, he placed his call, using a series of cutout codes to frustrate eavesdroppers. The telephone routing took him through a series of switchboards until he was connected with a familiar voice.

"Okay, Striker. What's up?"

"You've heard the news?"

"About the kid and the five dead hardcases? Yeah. What else?"

Bolan briefed Brognola on his encounter with Sonda Mgabe and his raid on the White Wolves' warehouse.

"BOSS has a manhunt going."

"I know. They're looking for a Mike Belasko. One of the Russians in their trade mission tipped us off. They think you're ex-CIA."

Bolan ignored the remark. "I need you to do some digging for information."

"What kind of information?"

"Tell me everything you can find out about Sonda Mgabe, a Major Pieter Volksmann of the Bureau of State Security and a man named Harry Desmond. Desmond's the one who provided the scholarships for Mgabe and her brother to study in the States. I'm curious how he fits into this puzzle."

The big Fed whistled. "Now he's world-class big-league. I know that much already. His ancestors discovered gold and diamond mines. Since then the Desmonds have controlled more money than the national banks of a lot of countries. With money comes power, and he's got lots of that, too."

"How fast can you send the information?"

"I'll fax it top priority before morning. It should be there tomorrow afternoon your time. Pick it up at the American Embassy under the Belasko name. It will be with the cultural attaché or one of his people."

"Cultural attaché? Does that mean CIA?"

"Well, let's just say you don't have to use pay phones, Striker. The phone in the apartment has been made secure."

ACROSS THE LOBBY, at the porter's desk, a stocky uniformed porter stared at Bolan, then studied a printed sheet of paper.

A red-faced Englishman, dressed in blazer and white linen pants, pulled the porter's arm.

"We're checking out. I'm going to need help with our luggage. We'll be in the dining room having tea."

"No problem," the porter replied with a smile. "If you could let me have your key, I will attend to it immediately."

The florid-faced visitor gave the man the key to his room and vanished through the dining-room doors. Reaching for the phone on his stand, the porter asked for an outside line, then dialed a number.

"This is Nathan. The man you want is making a call at a pay phone."

He hung up, picked up a luggage dolly and walked leisurely toward the elevators.

BOLAN SENSED that the hotel porter had been studying him. It didn't seem likely, but if the man had called the police, he had a choice of trying to escape by going back through the kitchen to his parked Audi or vanishing into the crowds on the street.

He loosened the suppressed Beretta 93-R in its shoulder rig. This was too public for someone to jump him, but Bolan had been attacked in more-crowded areas. Killers didn't care how many innocents got killed as long as they got their target.

Bolan decided to risk the streets. Moving quickly down the steps, he let the pedestrians swallow him.

He could feel eyes boring into his back. Slowly he turned. The porter hadn't emerged from the hotel.

If he was being paranoid, he kept reminding himself, even paranoids had enemies.

He noticed that a middle-aged man and woman standing near the entrance to the hotel were examining him. They whispered to each other, then vanished into the hotel lobby.

Paranoia or two of Volksmann's goons?

Bolan wasn't sure, but caution told him to get out of the area immediately. He'd pick up his car from behind the hotel later.

He spotted an empty cab traveling down Paul Kruger Street and hailed it.

The cab pulled over to the curb.

The driver smiled at him. "Taxicab, sir?"

Yanking the rear door open, Bolan started to jump inside—then saw the small black man sitting on the floor, pointing a Smith & Wesson .44 Magnum Model 29 at him.

"Get in, Mr. Belasko. Quickly, please," the man said.

More of Volksmann's hardmen? Hardly, he decided. The BOSS major wasn't likely to employ blacks. How did they know who he was?

Bolan thought of jumping back on the curb and spinning out of the way of any slugs.

"Harold also has a gun pointed at you," the man on the floor said. "Surely we won't both miss."

He knew the gunman was right.

As Bolan slid into the rear seat, he wondered who had sent the two men and how they had identified him.

He turned to the man to ask where they were going, but never got a chance.

He was blindsided, and everything went black as the gun in the man's hand slammed against the side of his head.

10

The room was half-underground. Only the row of narrow windows near the ceiling were at ground level.

The two young black men sat in wooden chairs and stared at the unconscious form chained to the heavy metal chair facing them.

The younger of the two turned to the other. "Should we get a doctor? He's been unconscious for more than an hour."

"No. She said to wait until he awakened by himself. She said he had a lot of stamina."

They turned their heads as the metal door squeaked. The woman who had opened it entered the room.

Sonda Mgabe crossed to the metal chair and examined Mack Bolan's head. Traces of blood still seeped from under the gauze pad taped over the wound on his temple.

"Mr. Belasko, are you awake?"

When he didn't move in response to her question, Sonda repeated it. Again and again she asked if he was awake.

Finally Bolan groaned, then blinked his eyes several times and eventually opened them.

Sonda's was the first face he saw, then the faces of the taxicab driver and the man in the backseat.

He closed his eyes against the throbbing in his head. "So you're the one who sent them."

"They had orders not to injure you unless you refused to go with them."

The throbbing refused to go away. "I don't remember them giving me a choice."

He tried to move his right hand to put pressure on the center of the pain, then realized his hands were chained behind his back.

"You came to South Africa at a bad time," she said coldly. "There is still a great deal of confusion and hatred as a result of the elections."

"I was invited here, if you remember, by your brother."

"If he hadn't asked for someone like you to come to our country, he might still be alive."

Bolan realized she didn't know that he was the one who had exposed the BOSS lie. He wasn't sure she would believe him if he told her that now.

In her eyes he was a white man. Therefore, nothing he said was the truth.

He stared back at her. "So what happens now?"

"We decide what to do with you."

Pulling over one of the wooden chairs, she sat and stared in his face.

"What do you know about our country, Mr. Belasko?"

"Only what I've read, and what I've seen since I've been here."

"What you've read was mostly written by white men. Let me enlighten you.

"Many years ago a powerful Zulu king named Shaka fought the Dutch and the British, and kept them from stealing our land, despite the fact that his troops had only spears and the white men had guns.

"Fifty years later another Zulu king named Cetshwayo decisively beat the British in the Anglo-Zulu War. Again the British used their superiority in guns and cannons to kill many Zulu warriors and their families."

"What about the other tribes?"

"Naturally they followed the lead of the Zulus and fought back as well as they could. In the end, the white man had to rely on his prisons, his armies and his weapons to enslave us."

Bolan wasn't interested in the history lesson. He turned his head and glanced at the small windows. All he could see was the darkening sky.

"Where exactly am I?"

"Is that important? You're on a farm in KwaZulu, the Zulu Homeland created by the white slavers."

"I have one more question."

The young woman looked annoyed. "What?"

"Why did you kidnap me?"

"We are checking your credentials, Mr. Belasko, to make sure you aren't working for the Bureau of State Security or one of the white terrorist gangs."

"I'm not," he replied bluntly. "What happens next?"

Sonda stared at him. "You will be notified."

"I thought you worked for the new government. But all you talk about are the Zulus."

"The government represents all blacks, as well as whites," she snapped, and strode out of the room.

The two men followed her out.

Alone, Bolan thought about the woman's speech. She sounded more like a Zulu missionary than someone advocating the rights of blacks. He wondered what group really owned her loyalty.

The Executioner looked around the damp, empty room. He knew he was in a tight spot. He suspected that the young woman was thinking of him as a scapegoat to get even with BOSS for trying to use her brother to discredit the black government. In his experience there were no causes so noble that their believers didn't resort to getting even with their enemies.

He wasn't sure how long the meeting to decide his fate would take. Meantime, he had to try to escape.

Getting his hands freed from the heavy chain that bound them to the chair would be a good beginning.

The chain was woven between the slats of the metal chair and cinched together with a padlock. He worked his fingers along the base of the slats.

From what he could feel, the damp basement had rusted the metal chair. His strong fingers kept pushing the slats forward and backward until he felt the metal edge of one of them. He wasn't certain how many more he needed to open, but he probably wouldn't be going anywhere in the near future.

Little by little he could feel the rusted slats surrender their soldered bond with the chair until finally they were all loosened.

Finding the right slats was a matter of trial and error. He wondered when somebody would return to the room and stop him.

Finally his chained wrists were free of the chair. He could stand, but his hands were still behind his back.

Bolan searched his memory for an idea, then remembered a magic show he had seen as a twelve-year-old. He'd been so fascinated by the stage magician that he'd cut classes three days in a row to watch him perform his act.

The trick that had fascinated him most was when the pretty girl who was the magician's assistant chained his hands behind his back with a pair of handcuffs, then helped him into a large trunk and closed the lid.

Within a few minutes, the lid of the trunk opened and the magician stepped out, his hands free.

When Bolan had gone backstage later, he kept asking how the performer had escaped. His persistence paid off. Finally the magician let him watch the trick, explaining it as he went along.

"Pull your legs tight against your body, then move your hands under your torso until they are in front. The rest is simple."

He opened his mouth and let Bolan look at the small key he had hidden under his tongue. "All you have to remember is to take the key with you into the trunk."

The Executioner didn't have a key. But he had an idea of how to get his hands on one if he could get his hands in front.

Lying on the ground, Bolan struggled to pull his legs against his body. The pain in his head kept interfering with his concentration.

Inch by inch he worked his hands down behind his legs, finally working the chain under his feet and in front.

Bolan spent a few moments stretching his cramped muscles, then sat in the chair and waited.

Minutes later the metal door swung open. A man entered, carrying a tray of food and a glass of water.

"I managed to get you some aspirin while you wait for Sonda to come back to talk to you. And something to eat."

He glanced at Bolan as he set the tray on the ground, then realized the large man no longer had his hands behind his back.

Reaching for the gun tucked in his waistband, the guard moved away from his captive. But Bolan was too fast. He pulled his chained hands over the head of the tray bearer, then pulled the chain hard against the man's throat.

Choking for air, the man struggled to get the pistol in his hand pointed at Bolan. But before he could, he collapsed into Bolan's arms, unconscious or dead.

Unconscious, the Executioner decided when he felt a weak pulse in the man's neck. He didn't kill unless it was absolutely necessary, and in this case his top priority was escaping, not killing.

If somebody interfered with his attempt to leave, that was a different matter.

Lowering the unconscious man to the floor, Bolan searched his pockets, found a key chain and looked through them until he found a key to the padlock.

After freeing himself, he took the gun from the man's limp right hand, then realized it was his own Beretta 93-R, still fitted with the silencer. He checked the clip and saw that it was still full.

He retrieved the three magazines the unconscious man had carried and shoved them into a pocket. Now it was time to get out of there.

Standing on his toes, he glanced out of one of the windows. It was deep dusk, and no one was in sight.

Another building, a large two-story structure, was two hundred yards away. Parked at its near side were two Land Rovers, the taxicab and a van. One of the keys on the guard's chain was for an ignition—to one of the Land Rovers, Bolan suspected. He hoped the darkening sky would mask his escape. The only weapon he had was the Beretta 93-R.

Resisting the temptation to chain the comatose captor to the chair, he opened the door and checked the corridor, which was empty.

With the Beretta leading the way, Bolan crept cautiously down the corridor, checking the doors on both sides as he went.

All the rooms were bare. Moving up the short flight of steps, he found himself in a large open area that led to a stout metal door.

Surveying the open area with a continuous sweep of his eyes, he padded to the door and opened it. Inside the small stone room he found an arms cache.

Cases of assault rifles, mostly Israeli Galils and Chinese AK-47s chambered for the same NATO rounds, were stacked next to several cases of semiautomatic pistols. A pair of World War II–vintage Browning .50 machine guns sat on tripods, next to three cases of ammo-filled ribbons for the weapons. The warrior had a healthy respect for the mini-cannons. They were still deadly no matter what their age.

A half-dozen M-72 A-2 LAWs were stacked next to cases of ammunition for the assault rifles and handguns.

Several cases of the British-made L-241 fragmentation grenades had been opened. And on the far side of the room, Bolan found two cases of British-made plastic explosive, and another case of detonators and timers to activate them.

From the markings on the boxes, Bolan knew that much of the inventory had come from Mozambique, where sympathizers were willing to help South African black activists destroy the white government.

Searching around, he found a large canvas carryall and started to fill it. A half-dozen blocks of the plastic explosive, as well as detonators and timers, were placed carefully on the bottom, then a dozen of the British grenades.

Bolan found his .44 Magnum Desert Eagle sitting on a wooden counter. Tucking the weapon into his waistband, he helped himself to a pair of Galil assault rifles, then searched for and found full clips for the weapon. Slapping full magazines into both weapons, he slung them over a shoulder.

He glanced at a pile of discarded leather holsters and spotted the Beretta shoulder rig and the Desert Eagle's waistband leather holster. Scooping them up, he shoved them into the bag.

The Executioner made one more sweep of the area. A small stack of cloth Zulu Action Front insignia caught his eye. The figure of a warrior holding a spear and the letters *ZAF* dominated the patch. He grabbed two and shoved them into the canvas bag.

As he planted bricks of plastique against the cases of ammo and explosives, and set the detonators and timers for ten minutes, he thought of the unconscious man locked in the cellar room.

He should survive the fireworks—unless he freed himself and decided to do something stupid like trying to find his former captive.

Grabbing the carryall, Bolan closed the metal door to the armory and catfooted to the door that led outside.

He swept a glance across the compound. Nobody was in sight. From the large house across the long yard, he could hear the sound of recorded music. Some American rock group was making more noise than music.

Bolan wasn't sure which vehicle would take the ignition key, so he tried the nearer of the two Land Rovers. The key fit. Tossing the carryall on the seat next to him, he got in and turned the key. The engine caught on the second try.

Reaching in the bag, Bolan took out a pair of delayed-action fragmentation grenades. He didn't need anyone chasing him. He backed out of the parking spot, then paused and pulled the pin on the grenade.

Hesitating only momentarily, he tossed the HE bomb at the second Land Rover and drove out of range before the grenade detonated and tore the vehicle apart.

Bolan pulled the pin on the second grenade and rolled it toward the van. The bomb vanished underneath the delivery vehicle, then exploded and lifted the delivery vehicle a foot in the air.

Two men raced out of the stone building, both armed.

Before either could get off a shot, Bolan leveled the Beretta and fired two rounds at the nearer gunner. The man flew backward, hit the side of the stone building and fell to the ground, clutching his lower left leg as blood spurted from his torn flesh.

The other man panicked. He triggered his pistol repeatedly, not counting on its recoil, and sent slugs in every direction.

Bolan heard the sound of a bullet ricocheting and ducked his head. A soft-nose slug chipped a corner of the Land Rover's windshield, and he returned fire hastily. The slugs tore through the upper muscle of the second man's leg, spinning him and slamming him into the building.

Other armed men poured out of the larger building and raised their weapons in the Executioner's direction. Then they froze and looked around to find the source of a muted rumbling.

The sequence inside the storage building started with small explosions, then kept getting louder as the roof tore open from the detonated plastique. Finally a multicolored display of fireworks shot into the sky as the central inventory of cases of ammo and explosives ignited.

The group stared in fear and awe at the loud, brilliant show across the yard, which threatened to blind them and shatter their eardrums at the same time. Bolan took advantage of the distraction, slammed his vehicle into gear and raced away from the farm.

11

Reggie Mgabe took off his police constable's cap and mopped his sweating forehead with a paper napkin.

The stout black waitress recognized him.

"*Molo,* Reggie. You alone today?"

"Good morning to you, too, Martha. Constable Jennings said he'd meet me for lunch." He loosened his uniform shirt collar and followed the waitress to an empty booth. "Damned hot outside," he complained. "Even for Soweto."

A large fan fought futilely to dispel the heat in the plainly furnished lunchroom.

"Not much better in here," she replied. "Maybe you should ask your niece for a national government job. She must be doing well. At least you'd get an air-conditioned office."

"Getting a scholarship to an American university didn't hurt her employment chances," the constable replied. "Me, I didn't even get to finish school. That's why I became a township constable instead of joining the South African police."

He leaned back in the rickety wooden chair and sighed, like old men do.

"No, I wish Sonda well, but I've got a pension coming up in a few years. I don't want to throw that away for some temporary fancy job with the government."

The waitress smiled and handed him a food-stained menu. "Coffee while you wait?"

"May as well."

His shift was barely half-over, and it already felt as if he'd worked overtime. With gangs like the Boasters and the confrontations between the various activist groups, Soweto had become a dangerous place.

As he stirred the two large spoonfuls of sugar he'd put in the coffee cup, Reggie Mgabe heard the front door open and looked up.

He recognized the frail old man who entered—Dr. Abel Methabane. The constable knew that he was more than just another Soweto Township doctor. He'd heard about the secret meetings being held in the doctor's home.

Methabane looked around and seemed surprised to see the officer. He walked over and slid onto the torn plastic seat facing him.

"Hot one out there, Reggie," he said.

The constable glanced at his uninvited guest through suspicion-filled eyes. "A two-shirt day, Doctor," the cop agreed. Then he asked, "What brings you out of your infirmary?"

"A pregnant woman who can't come to me to help her deliver her baby. We haven't seen you at a meeting for a long time, Reggie."

The constable shook his head. "I'm not one for politics. Especially with the election over and done with."

"Your niece is," Methabane replied smoothly.

Reggie Mgabe's expression revealed his unhappiness. Since her parents died, Sonda had been a student of the elderly doctor. She had quoted his philosophy about everything. Sometimes Mgabe wondered if the doctor had hypnotized her.

The constable reluctantly agreed. "The government got a bright one when they hired her."

"And your nephew," the doctor added.

Reggie Mgabe's face reflected his sorrow. "Damn the butchers who murdered him!"

"Bureau of State Security men. Policemen," the elderly man reminded him. "And the new government hasn't seen fit to put them out of business."

The constable nodded, then lifted his coffee cup and sipped silently.

The doctor looked around to make sure no one was listening, then leaned over and spoke in a low voice. "We could use a friend inside your department. Someone we can trust."

Reggie looked out of his window and saw two men walking rapidly toward the lunchroom.

"Not me. I don't like your other friends."

Methabane seemed puzzled, then joined the constable in looking out the window.

A tall black man, with three parallel scars carved about his right eye, and another thick-bodied man, similarly marked, were heading his way.

The constable recognized both of them. Lucas Tsombe, head of the Boasters, and one of his men, a thug named Big Joseph.

Like most police officers in the black township, he knew a lot about the Boasters. A gang of hustlers, extortionists, hired killers and drug dealers, they terrorized the streets of the segregated communities that surrounded Johannesburg. Their self-inflicted facial scars reflected their absurd pride in being members of the gang.

Their leader had a nickname—"Inyoka," which meant "snake" in Zulu. It fit Tsombe. He was dangerous, and a killer. He'd been arrested for a variety of crimes, but his expensive lawyers always managed to get the charges dismissed.

Reggie was bitter about the marijuana and tranquilizers from India that were being smuggled into the country and channeled down to street addicts through gangs like the Boasters. "Until somebody cuts off their supply of drugs," he had constantly complained to other officers, "they'll keep robbing, murdering and pushing their Mandrax and Dagga."

Reggie dropped some change onto the table and called out to the waitress. "Tell Jennings I had to leave."

Bad timing, Methabane thought. He hadn't expected Sonda's uncle to be here. He watched as the constable shoved past the pair entering the lunchroom.

Tsombe looked around, saw the doctor and joined him in the booth. The other man waited at the door, one hand under his loose-fitting jacket.

The Boasters' chief sounded annoyed. "Talking to coppers now, Doctor?"

"I talk to anyone who wishes to talk to me, Lucas. You called and asked if I would meet you. Why?"

Tsombe leaned forward and spoke softly. "We're running low on supplies."

Methabane smiled. "Then I assume that this is a business meeting. I was hoping that as a man of Zulu descent you were finally willing to help us achieve our destiny."

The elderly doctor remembered the brief meeting with Harry Desmond. Finding a Zulu willing to sacrifice his life to eliminate the new president would bring a substantial contribution to the Zulu Action Front he controlled.

Lucas Tsombe was the perfect choice.

"No fancy talk," the Boasters' head whispered, stopping the Zulu Action Front leader. "I need goods to sell. How quick can you get them to me?"

Methabane sighed. There was always Sonda. He'd thought about Tsombe's question.

"Drop in at the infirmary around ten tomorrow night. I should have an answer for you."

Tsombe nodded. "I'll be there." He stood, then walked to the front door, signaled his bodyguard and left the lunchroom.

THE UNIFORMED POLICE officer was straightening his immaculate jacket as Tsombe entered the abandoned Soweto shop that served as his headquarters. The Boasters' leader looked around. The place was empty, except for the two of them.

"You're late," Major Volksmann said, checking his wristwatch.

"I knew you'd wait," the Boasters' chief replied without concern. He moved to the small, battered desk set against a wall and sat on it. "Why did you want to see me?"

The major leaned against a nearby wall. "There was no payment from you this week," he replied coldly. "Our agreement is that there will be a payment of two thousand rand each week. This means you will owe me four thousand rand next week."

Tsombe toyed with the idea of killing the BOSS officer, then changed his mind. The arrangement had been mutually beneficial. In exchange for a weekly sum, the Bureau of State Security ignored complaints about the Boasters.

"You'll get your money," Lucas Tsombe promised. "Right now I'm arranging to get another shipment delivered."

Volksmann checked his watch again. He started to leave, then remembered something.

"If your men happen to run into this man—" he extracted a folded sheet of paper from an inner pocket and handed it to Tsombe "—there's a reward for his capture."

Tsombe studied the sketch. "Who is he?"

"A paid assassin. An American. He killed some of my men when they weren't looking," the major replied glibly.

"How much?"

"Enough to cover last week's and this week's fees."

The Boasters' chieftain glanced at the sketch again, then smiled at Volksmann.

"We'll find him for you."

12

Bolan's head and shoulder still throbbed, but the pain was beginning to subside. He was glad to be back in the relative security of his Pretoria safehouse.

He hadn't been to bed yet, but he needed a shower and a cup of strong coffee more than he needed sleep.

Stripping off his clothes, he moved into the bathroom and turned on the shower full blast. He watched as steam filled the tile-walled room and was grateful that the landlord provided lots of hot water.

Stepping under the nozzle, he let the scorching spray beat on his aching head and body. As he let the hot water relieve his tortured muscles, he thought about the trip back.

It had been a long drive along foggy rural roads, looking for a gas station or someone who could give him directions. But nothing had been open, and the roads were deserted.

As he had made his way through the darkened terrain, his vision was reduced to the fifty feet around him. Potholes in the roads had made driving difficult.

Then a bus had appeared suddenly out of the thick mist, moving toward him. The sign above the driver's window had read Pretoria. Executing a quick U-turn, Bolan had followed the vehicle.

It was dawn before familiar landmarks had begun to appear.

The streets were empty when he pulled behind the Victoria Hotel and parked the Land Rover. The Audi 500 was still there, a parking ticket pushed under one of the wiper blades.

Picking up the canvas carryall, he abandoned the Land Rover, switched to the Audi, then drove around the corner to Paul Kruger Street.

Two men loitering in front of the hotel looked as if they'd been up all night. They looked like street thugs the world over, big, with lots of muscle. One was burly and surly faced. The other was built like a Japanese sumo wrestler.

Bolan wasn't sure if they were with BOSS or members of one of the terrorist armies. Not that it mattered.

The surly faced thug spotted him and dragged his partner to a nearby parked car, a Ford Anglia, to give chase.

Bolan stomped on the accelerator and roared around a corner, wondering how they had made him. Had the BOSS major gotten hold of an accurate description?

He checked his rearview mirror and saw the burly hood in the passenger seat of the Ford. He poked a 7.62 mm Valmet M-76 assault rifle out of his opened window. A short burst of hardball NATO rounds from the Finnish gun's 30-round magazine tore chunks of metal out of the Audi's trunk.

The Executioner began an evasive maneuver, weaving his car from left to right across the road.

Hoping to put distance between himself and his pursuers, Bolan approached an oncoming corner at racing speed. He twisted the wheel hard toward the inside of the curb and tapped the brakes just enough to put the Audi into a slide. The rear of the vehicle swung to the outside. As he executed a neat four-wheel drift, he shoved the gearshift to low, stomped on the accelerator and shot out of the curb. He could hear the tires of the Ford behind him squeal as the driver skidded and spun out, trying to maneuver through the same turn at high speed.

Reaching into the canvas bag on the floor, Bolan reached for the Galil AR he had appropriated and three spare clips loaded with 7.62 mm rounds.

He maintained the pattern of erratic short turns in the narrow road until he saw a sidewalk café, closed until afternoon, ahead.

Metal tables and chairs were stacked against the brick building that supported its awning. He decided to make his stand there and spun the Audi onto the sidewalk.

As the car crashed through the furniture, Bolan grabbed the Galil and spare clips, and opened the car door. Just before the vehicle came to a complete stop against a wall, he jumped from the Audi.

The driver of the car behind hadn't expected the sudden stop and jammed on his brakes. The Ford skidded, then smashed into Bolan's rented car.

The Executioner took refuge behind the front hood of the battle-scarred Audi, then watched the surly faced hit man force his way out of the Ford. Nervously he sprayed a continuous burst of rounds at Bolan's car to cover his exit, then dived behind the door of the Ford.

The Valmet's hammer hit metal, and Bolan could hear the shooter desperately try to ram another magazine into the assault rifle.

The driver took advantage of his partner's action and worked his rotund body out of the small car. A 7.62 mm Tokarev pistol filled his fleshy hand, and he crouched behind the driver's door of the small car, using it as a shield.

Bolan wanted to end the battle peaceably, if possible. The pair of thugs could be a valuable source of information.

"Drop the guns," he shouted.

"Drop dead, American," the burly thug holding the assault rifle shouted back in accented English.

He had called out to the driver.

"You with the Tokarev. Is that how you feel?"

"*Ja.*" Then, in a show of bravado, he popped up and loosed five rounds at Bolan's position.

Bolan was no longer there, having moved to the right after shouting the surrender order.

He decided the time for conversation was over. Bolan waited for the Valmet shooter to raise his head again. When the surly faced hit man did, the Executioner unleashed a 3-round burst of 7.62 mm death from the Galil. He could hear the thud of a body banging into metal behind the passenger door.

Without warning, the burly rifleman stood, his face twisted by anger, and loosed a barrage of lead in Bolan's direction.

Blood pouring from a shoulder wound, the gunner started to walk toward Bolan.

Surprised at the man's false courage, the Executioner waited until his target man got closer, then loosed a trio of 7.62 mm slugs.

The soft noses tore into the rifleman's chest and neck. As if he were impervious to bullets, the man had kept moving forward.

Bolan knew the hardman was fatally wounded, but he didn't believe in taking unnecessary risks.

He released another two rounds. The impact spun the shooter and slammed him back into the door of his car. He dropped his weapon and slid to the ground.

Bolan turned his attention to the second gunner, who had watched his partner die. The hardman kept darting up from behind the Ford, punctuating his appearances with bursts of 7.62 mm lead. Two slugs tore into the Audi, shattering a side window.

Bolan had moved away from the rental car and dropped to the ground. He began to elbow his way toward the other vehicle and heard the gunman clicking a new clip into his Tokarev.

The hit man raised his head again and looked around, trying to spot his target.

Bolan triggered a pair of rounds at the exposed face, drilling holes through the gunman's nose and cheek and carving a passage to his brain.

The big American heard the clatter of his adversary's gun as it struck the ground. He waited a few moments, then moved cautiously to the Ford.

The hit man had fallen behind the driver's door. What was left of his face was a huge cavity, leaking blood and tissue. His partner was also dead, his body hidden behind the bullet-punctured passenger door.

Bolan searched through the driver's pockets and found a wallet. Inside was a membership card for the AWB, which the Executioner pocketed. The two dead men had obviously been recruited for this assignment.

He had a thick file on the neofascist group. The AWB was one of the most fanatic of the white militant organizations. But who had gotten them to volunteer? The only name that came to Bolan's mind was Pieter Volksmann. He had to have gotten tired of losing his own men and found a pair of fanatics to take their places.

Bolan didn't waste time mourning the dead. They had signed their death warrants when they decided to do a favor for Volksmann.

He dropped the notice of the Order of Death rally near the Ford. It should create some questions about who was responsible for the two deaths.

He walked back to the demolished Audi, retrieved the canvas carryall and walked back to where he had parked the Land Rover.

13

Refreshed after a ten-minute soaking under the hot, piercing spray, Bolan stepped out of the shower, toweled himself dry and slipped into a pair of shorts. At least some of the fatigue had vanished.

He needed coffee and hoped the tenant had left some behind.

Searching the cupboards, he found a canister of instant coffee in the cabinet over the sink. Bolan set a kettle of cold water on the stove and switched the knob to high.

Turning on the television set, he changed channels until he came to World News—the international cable news outlet. A smartly dressed woman was summarizing the national headlines.

"Regarding the murder of Kenneth Mgabe at the Voortrekker Monument, a spokesman for the Bureau of State Security said that his department was investigating all possibilities. He added that they'd received a tip the young Zulu man had been killed by members of the Zulu-dominated Inkatha Freedom Party.

"Turning to other news," the woman reporter continued, "two residents of Pretoria were found shot to death on a side street this morning. A source within the South African police blamed the murders on the increasing violence in the country, since the new government took office."

Bolan wondered if the police told the press about the rally notice he had left behind.

"Rivalry among the right-wing gangs exploded today. Members of the AWB, the White Wolves and several other terrorist organizations clashed on the streets of a number of cities in South Africa. Each accused the others of trying to kill their members. Police flying squads rushed in before the fistfights turned the streets into a war zone."

The Executioner assumed the police had told the groups of the announcements they had found.

"Several members of the organizations were taken into custody for carrying concealed loaded weapons."

Bolan wasn't surprised that no mention was made of the destroyed warehouse. It wasn't the kind of news that the groups wanted released. His campaign was having an effect. No coalition of the groups had been formed. At least, not yet. He had to make sure none did.

He was about to turn off the set when something the newscaster was saying caught his ear.

"This announcement was just handed to me. The president of South Africa said that in a effort to bring about reconciliation of the various ethnic groups in the country, he would address a large rally at Soccer City in Turffontein, just outside of Johannesburg, next Saturday morning. This despite reported threats to assassinate him.

"The government leader said that if twenty years in prison didn't frighten him, mere threats wouldn't, either. The rally is expected to attract as many as one hundred thousand."

"This is Judith Thompson with World News."

As he turned off the television set, Bolan shook his head. It was as if the man had a death wish. He'd be a sitting duck.

The phone rang, and Bolan answered it.

"I heard about the rally," Hal Brognola said without preamble. "We can talk about that another time."

What bothered the Executioner was how willing the elderly man was to speak at any public rally, large or small, with little or no protection.

How to keep the new president alive was a serious dilemma.

"You wanted detailed information on Harry Desmond and two other people. An envelope for you should be at the embassy by now." The big Fed paused, then added, "You might want to know that one of Desmond's people bought a couple of planeloads of arms and other similar goodies from a dealer in Angola. They'll ship it via Mozambique."

Bolan was surprised, not that Brognola had gotten the information, but that someone as rich as Desmond would want to buy that many arms.

For the moment his concerns about the safety of the South African president were set aside by his friend's news.

"I thought Desmond was a world-class good guy."

"I've changed my mind," the big Fed replied in a flat tone.

Bolan didn't press the issue. There was too much else to discuss. "Delivery when and where?"

"Just across the border."

"Anything more specific about date and place?"

"We paid enough to find out what color shorts the crews would be wearing. The White Wolves are picking it up." He paused, then asked, "You don't happen to have a map of the border handy?"

"I can make notes," Bolan said as he searched for paper and pen.

Brognola gave him the precise coordinates for the landing field. "Delivery is scheduled for tomorrow night just after midnight."

"Anything out of the ordinary coming in?"

"Aside from assault rifles, handguns and ammo, nothing much. Just some M-72 A-2 LAWs loaded with 66 mm HEAT warheads, capable of penetrating 200 mm armor, plastic explosives and detonators. That sort of thing."

Bolan had a healthy respect for LAWs. The hand-held rocket launcher was a throwaway weapon that could be fitted with anything from a fragmentation missile to a small nuclear warhead.

"Sounds like a good opportunity to get rid of some killing machines and continue creating distrust among the groups," Bolan declared.

"You've done a good job so far," Brognola commented. "I got a report about the warehouse explosion last night. I figured it was you when State Department Intel reported that the cops had found a notice about some antigovernment rally from a rival group."

Bolan thought of the membership card he had lifted last night from the dead man's wallet. Leaving a piece of it at the delivery site would raise a few eyebrows. If anyone was still alive to raise anything after he got done.

"Thanks. I think I've got a topper to that," he said, then signed off.

He slipped into a loose-fitting sport shirt, a pair of khaki wash pants, socks and loafers. Then heard the kettle start to whistle. He still needed the cup of coffee to help him snap his mind into high gear.

Spooning the prebrewed powder into a large porcelain cup, he filled the cup with steaming water, added some of the powdered cream he had found in the cupboard and stirred the mixture.

He propped up the pillows on the bed, sat against them and sketched out the day's schedule in his head. A visit to the American Embassy was high on his list. So was getting ready to meet the arms shipment at the border with Mozambique.

As he reflected on what to bring with him across the border, he heard a sound at the door. Someone was inserting a key.

Grabbing the silenced Beretta 93-R from under his pillow, he rolled onto the floor.

The door swung open, and Bolan tightened his finger on the trigger as he aimed at the opening entrance.

Sonda Mgabe stepped inside the room. She held a finger to her lips before he could speak and closed the door behind her.

"There are four men waiting outside. Two in front and two at the rear," she announced calmly as Bolan lowered his gun.

"BOSS?"

She shook her head. "More likely AWB storm troopers. At least they're wearing those swastika-style patches on their sleeves."

Bolan wasn't sure he believed her. "How would they know where I was here?"

"The same way I found you. They must have shown a sketch of you around."

She handed him a folded sheet of paper. The warrior opened it and studied the face that stared back at him. There was a strong likeness.

Sonda Mgabe smiled patiently. "The police artist must have gotten your description from the agent at the airport who rented you the car."

Bolan remembered the wispy little man who had stared at him from over the car-rental counter.

"He helps out BOSS," the young woman explained, "in exchange for their ignoring his frequent incursions into the black townships in search of women to share his bed."

"I guess it's time to move."

"Even getting to the Land Rover parked behind the building will be a problem," she warned.

Bolan took his hardware into the bathroom and closed the door. He was reluctant to let the young woman see what he carried and where.

He slipped into the shoulder rig and holstered the suppressed Beretta 93-R. The Desert Eagle was tucked into his waistband, and finally he strapped a Ka-bar combat knife to his forearm. A loose-fitting lightweight jacket covered everything.

Coming out of the bathroom, Bolan hastily opened dresser drawers and closet doors. Grabbing clothing and the rest of his personal belongings, he stuffed them into an overnight bag. Then he picked up the bag and the two canvas carryalls that held his gear, and headed for the front door.

He wasn't sure where he'd go, but it was obvious he couldn't stay there.

But first came dealing with the thugs downstairs. Quickly he improvised a plan of action.

"Open the door and walk in front of me," he ordered, "and keep your hands where I can see them."

She nodded and followed his orders.

As they moved down the stairs to the ground floor, Bolan asked if she'd come in a car.

"It's parked out front," she replied, nodding.

"Good. I want you to run out of the building yelling that a man tried to rape you. That should get the attention of the two out front. Then get in your car and drive away."

"I'm black," she reminded him. "Why would they care?"

"Just do it," he ordered.

He set down his bags and waited on the steps until he heard her yelling. As he suspected they would, the two hit men waiting in the back of the building ran inside, curious what the female voice was shouting.

Bolan slipped the Ka-bar knife from its sheath and waited until the first of the uniformed pair passed by him. Then he grabbed the second man around the chest and, with a smooth slashing movement, cut him deeply across the stomach.

He released his adversary and let him slide to the ground, staining the light wood with his blood.

The first hardman turned back at his companion's cries of pain, but most of his attention was caught by the Beretta's unwavering muzzle.

"Time to give up," Bolan said quietly. Maybe he could find out who had sent the two teams.

The hardman was either too stupid or too stubborn to comply with Bolan's order. Whipping out a SIG-Sauer P-226 from its waistband holster, the thug tried to point the weapon at the warrior.

Two muffled 9 mm parabellum rounds from Bolan's gun ripped through the skin of the hit man's throat and were deflected upward to his brain before he could squeeze the trigger.

The dying neofascist tried to mouth a curse as he slowly sank to the ground, but death claimed him before he could say anything.

There were still two more out front. But Bolan decided he didn't need to get into a shooting contest with so many innocent pedestrians walking on the street.

He reached into a pocket and, near the bodies, dropped one of the insignia he had found at the White Wolves' weapons depot.

Sliding the knife back into its sheath and the Beretta into its rigid shoulder pocket, he picked up his bags and headed for the back door.

Sonda had driven to the rear of the building. She was waiting for him by her car.

He ignored her as he placed his bags in the Land Rover.

Getting into his surplus vehicle, Bolan started the engine, then turned to the young woman.

He was curious. "What made you look for me?"

"To apologize for yesterday. You might not believe this, but removing you from Pretoria was partly for your own good."

"Thanks," Bolan replied sarcastically, then touched his still-sore temple and winced. "I could say the same about eliminating your weapons depot."

She was about to snap an angry reply, then changed her mind.

"I am sorry we had to render you unconscious. There was no other way to have you come with our men."

"What's this 'for my own good' business?"

"Major Volksmann has had every member of the bureau in Pretoria and Jo'burg out on the streets looking for you. The orders were that if they couldn't capture you, they were to kill you."

"Isn't there anybody in this country who is innocent of trying to kill some white or black?"

The young woman shook her head. "These are not innocent times."

Bolan nodded in agreement. There was no total innocence anywhere in the world. That was why he continued doing what he did.

"So keeping me away from harm was the reason you had me kidnapped."

"Not exactly." She hesitated, then continued, "We were also discussing a proper response to the stupid attempt to blame blacks for bombing the Boer monument."

"Like what?"

"Like having a black landmark destroyed by explosives and leaving your body to be found among the ruins."

"Too obvious," Bolan commented.

"The council thought so, too. We—they—decided that you might be more valuable to us alive. I was driving back from the meeting to have the men return you to Pretoria when I heard the explosions and saw you drive off."

"How are your men?"

"Alive. They are all wearing casts and bragging to everyone that they had been wounded in combat." She paused, then added, "Thank you for not killing them."

Bolan nodded. "That wasn't my intention."

She looked as though she understood. Then she opened her purse. Bolan pointed the Beretta at her. Ignoring the weapon, she reached into the handbag and took out a box of cigarettes and a lighter.

She lit a cigarette and returned the box and lighter to her purse.

"Perhaps we can work together," she suggested.

She seemed to be friendlier, which aroused his curiosity. "Why the sudden willingness to be helpful?"

"I heard that a large American had provided the television newspeople and other representatives of the press with copies of the autopsy report that proved that Kenny had been murdered. I'm surprised you didn't save it for an exclusive story," she commented.

"Some stories need to be shared with the competition."

"Is there anything you need?"

He thought for a moment.

"Information."

"If you don't mind being seen in public with a black woman, we can have dinner and discuss it then."

Bolan agreed. Sonda suggested a restaurant in Pretoria.

"Eight?"

"I'll be there," he promised.

"Meantime, I suggest you find a different place to live."

He waved in agreement as he drove away to pick up the envelope he knew was waiting for him at the American Embassy.

14

The familiar red, white and blue flag fluttered in the breeze, suspended from a tall white pole in front of the handsome white building on Pretoria Street.

Knowing he would have to clear the security monitoring system at the Embassy entrance, Mack Bolan had locked the Beretta 93-R in the glove compartment of the Land Rover and parked it down the street.

He walked past the Marine guard, and, once inside the vast lobby, he looked around. A circular staircase led up to the next level. Ornately carved doors covered both side walls, while a large series of curtained windows filled the rear of the lobby. In the center was a circular counter. The neatly dressed young woman who sat behind it watched as Bolan walked toward her.

Smiling at him, she asked, "How can I help you, sir?"

"You're holding an envelope for Mike Belasko."

Still smiling, she typed the name on the keyboard of her computer. When words appeared on the monitor, her expression became businesslike. She lifted the receiver on the telephone nearby and dialed a number.

"Mike Belasko is here."

Replacing the receiver, she turned to Bolan. "Mr. Preston of the cultural-affairs staff will be right down."

The Executioner turned away and studied the paintings on the lobby walls. Framed portraits of Presidents and former ambassadors were abundant. Typical bureaucratic interior decorating, Bolan decided.

A serious-faced young man in a dark business suit walked swiftly down the stairs and approached him.

"I'm Jay Preston. If you'll follow me, Mr. Belasko."

The young Embassy executive led the way down the carpeted hallway to an office door and opened it. He led the way inside, then closed the door. Moving behind the desk, he reached into a drawer and withdrew a manila envelope covered with official-looking seals. "I believe this is what you want."

Bolan took the envelope from Preston's hand and turned to leave.

The young staffer stopped him. "Got a minute?"

"What's on your mind?" Bolan asked as he faced the man.

Preston eased into the swivel chair. "You know that BOSS is looking for an American reporter named Mike Belasko."

He pointed to a chair in front of his desk, and Bolan accepted the offer.

"What else is new?"

"You must have really gotten them mad. They've been keeping a low profile since the election."

Bolan thought of the numerous BOSS thugs he'd eliminated so far, as well as their neofascist colleagues.

"Just the preliminary rounds."

Preston smiled. "We contacted the rental agency and let them know your car had been stolen. The insurance should cover the damage when they find it."

Bolan was impressed. Preston was part of a new breed.

"Is 'cultural affairs' the new cover title?"

Preston ignored the question. "Somebody in the United States talked to the people in Langley about lending a hand if necessary. They contacted my boss down here...you know the routine. Officially we can't get involved in local politics."

It was obvious to Bolan that the sincere-sounding man hadn't been aboard long enough to become cynical.

"That's why I'm here."

"For the record we don't know you exist. So we can't help you." He paused, then lowered his voice. "Off the record there are a lot of people who used to be in power who shouldn't be walking the streets."

Bolan understood. "It's soon going to be time for Mike Belasko, American reporter, to vanish," he replied. "I operate better when I don't have to wear a jacket that's uncomfortable."

The young government agent smiled, then became serious. "Can I ask you a question?"

Bolan nodded. "If you want."

"Did you ever get to meet Kenneth Mgabe?"

"He'd been picked up by the goon squad before I got there."

"You would have liked him. I met him when he came to the States," Preston reminisced. "I was in my senior year and he was bewildered by everything." He hesitated. "I took him under my wing. A good human being. Someone who loved people. Not just blacks, but all people. All he ever wanted to do was go back to his country, expose the people who were profiting from the violence and try to get the various groups to work out a compromise."

Bolan pondered the words. *Compromise.* That was all Kenny Mgabe had wanted, according to the Embassy staffer.

Something clicked. That was what was wrong with this country. Everyone wanted everything or nothing.

From what he remembered about American history, the United States wouldn't have happened with that attitude. There had been a lot of give and take even among the Founding Fathers. If only the blacks and whites in South Africa would follow that example, local undertakers would have a lot less business.

It was a thought worth pursuing. But not now. He had other priorities.

"Time to get out of here," Bolan commented, making a move to stand up.

"Hold on half a second," Preston said.

Turning his back on the warrior, the government staffer opened a door in his credenza and took out a package.

He handed it to Bolan and commented, "Kenny asked me to hang on to this for him until he could come and retrieve it." He looked sad as he stared at the taped brown manila parcel. "He won't be retrieving it."

Bolan wondered if this was the missing evidence. He looked at the young man behind the desk. "Care to see what's inside?"

The cultural-affairs officer looked uncertain. "As a representative of the United States government, I don't think I should—"

The Executioner stopped him. "As Kenneth Mgabe's friend, you should."

Jay Preston lifted his hands in surrender, then reached into his center drawer. He handed Bolan a pair of scissors.

The Executioner slit the parcel open. There was a stack of photocopies inside and a handwritten list.

He handed it to the young man. "Mgabe's handwriting?"

Preston studied the piece of paper. "I think so."

Meantime, Bolan thumbed through the pages, emitting a soft whistle as he did.

"If this was the United States," he commented, "a lot of people in high places would be going to jail."

Preston was curious. "What did he copy?"

"Bank transfers. Bank deposits. Memos." He gave one of the copied memos a quick reading.

"There's enough here to prove that a lot of important men in this country have been involved in the systematic murders of blacks and whites who didn't agree with their philosophies."

He slammed a photocopied stack of pages on Preston's desk, then pointed to the top one.

"That person is offering top dollar to anyone who can kill the new president."

The Embassy staffer glanced at the page. "He was a cabinet minister in the previous administration. And here are payoffs to senior military and police officials to turn their heads when one of the terrorist groups attacks one of the ethnic groups."

Preston kept thumbing through the stack.

"Here's a half-dozen transfers to a Swiss bank account from Harry Desmond." He added the totals on the transfer forms. "More than two million rand. That's close to a million dollars in our money."

Bolan shook his head as he looked across the desk. "Have that Swiss account checked out. But you can bet it belongs to someone who was way up in the government." He stared at the field agent. "How did Mgabe get all of this?"

Preston looked bewildered. "I don't know. Kenny had a lot of friends—white, as well as black—who believed that with a new president it was time things really changed in this country. Maybe they helped him gather it."

"How about his sister? Do you think she knew?"

"Sonda?"

Bolan didn't miss the expression on Preston's face. It was one of regret.

"I don't think so. She always said that she was the fighter in the family," Preston answered.

"There's a lot about her that bothers me. For one thing, does her government job pay well?"

Preston shrugged. "I don't think anybody over there gets paid well."

"She can afford a relatively new car and nice clothes for someone without much money. Who else does she work for?"

"I don't know."

Bolan shot another question at the young Embassy staffer. "She talks a lot about the Zulus. Why?"

"That's her heritage."

"Do the security officials know that?"

"You'll have to ask them."

"Any chance of checking it out?"

"I can try," Preston promised. The young man hesitated, then added, "There was a time when I thought we—" He stopped and changed the subject. "I'll ask around and see if anyone knows anything more about her."

"The sooner the better. Tension isn't likely to ease in the near future," Bolan warned.

"I know," Preston said. It was obvious to Bolan that Preston was worried about something.

"I don't know who you are, Mr. Belasko, but you've made some powerful enemies in the short time you've been here. People like Major Pieter Volksmann are used to getting their own way in South Africa."

Bolan flashed a cold smile. "Things are changing in this country. I got a feeling Volksmann is on the way out."

He gathered up the photocopies and stood.

"Some advice," Preston offered. "I wouldn't go back to the apartment. The men who were looking for you had friends. Some of them are sure to be waiting for you."

Bolan nodded in agreement. "I've got my gear in the car downstairs. I could use a new place."

Preston reached into a pocket, took out a key and handed it over, saying, "I have a small apartment in Johannesburg that I use when I want to get away for a weekend."

"Thanks." Bolan meant it.

The Agency representative scribbled the address on the top page of a small pad and passed it to him.

"Let me know when it's safe for me to use again."

15

Bolan spotted them when he walked up the street from the American Embassy: two young white men in jeans and thin leather jackets loitering near the Land Rover.

He ignored them and got into the vehicle.

The men stared at a sketch on a sheet of paper, then looked at him. Without a word they mounted a parked Vespa scooter and pulled away from the curb.

The Executioner started the engine, released the brake, turned the wheel hard and shifted into second. The vintage Land Rover squealed in complaint as he raced it down the street past them. Then he shifted into third gear and accelerated.

If the pair was following him, Bolan decided he'd lead them on a chase they wouldn't forget.

Threading his way through the heavy traffic in central Pretoria, Bolan narrowly missed a bus as he whipped into Bosman Street. He ignored shaken fists and shouted curses and kept his eyes peeled for openings in the endless parade of vehicles and pedestrians crowding across the intersections.

In his rearview mirror he could see the Vespa's driver pumping fuel in an effort to keep up with him. The narrow scooter could have inched through openings in the traffic, but the driver seemed to be satisfied staying behind the Land Rover.

Bolan knew that someplace ahead were the rail yards, a good place to take a stand without involving innocent pedestrians. He visualized the map of the city in his mind and worked out a route to get there.

With his hand jamming the Land Rover's horn, he maneuvered around trucks and passenger cars that threatened to crash into him. Pedestrians, startled by the horn, jumped back on the sidewalks as he crossed Schoeman, then Skinner Street.

A woman crossing with a baby carriage forced him to slam on the brakes. While he waited, he opened the glove compartment and grabbed the Beretta and placed it on the seat next to him.

He could see the passenger on the Vespa whispering into the driver's ear. Suddenly the driver sped up and tried to close the gap between his vehicle and the Land Rover. A group of schoolchildren crossing the street scattered as the Italian-made scooter plowed toward them in its relentless pursuit of its target.

Bolan's vehicle jumped the curb and moved around a small crowd, which scrambled out of the way as he approached. His combat senses tingled, letting him know his pursuers were about to make their play, and he wanted to get as far away from onlookers as he could before they did.

The Vespa raced onto the sidewalk behind him. An elderly man was knocked to the ground as he tried to move out of the path of the motor scooter. Several people rushed to his aid and helped him to his feet.

Bolan resigned himself to the situation. The battle was going to take place before he could reach the rail yards. He glanced over his shoulder and saw the passenger release his grip on the driver's waist and aim an odd-looking weapon.

He recognized the gun—the Striker 12. Drug dealers called it the Street Sweeper, and Bolan had seen gang members use it back in the States. Then he remembered that they were manufactured in South Africa. The gun had been developed for "crowd control" of a brutal and bloody sort.

A cross between a shotgun and a large revolver, the Striker 12 could release a dozen shotgun shells from its coffee-can-shaped magazine in a few seconds. What it lacked in accuracy, it made up for in killing power.

In most hands the weapon was impossible to control. If fired from the shoulder, the powerful recoil would overcome any but the most massively built shooters. The thugs that stuck with the gun always fired it from the hip.

The Executioner grabbed the Beretta and turned briefly to fire, but there were too many civilians around for him to risk shooting.

The Land Rover scraped a fender along the wall, creating a trail of sparks. Bolan steered the vehicle around another baby carriage and back into the roadway. The driver of the Vespa followed close behind, oblivious to the panic he was creating.

Temporarily stymied, his passenger lowered his weapon and wrapped a hand around the driver's waist. Twenty yards later traffic closed in and forced both Bolan and the Vespa's driver to use their brakes.

Bolan looked back and saw the rider pointing the Street Sweeper again. As the shooter pulled on the trigger, the warrior ducked to the floor. Two rounds of shotgun slugs shattered the left half of the Land Rover's windshield.

The Executioner snapped a pair of shots at the Vespa. One missed and tore into the asphalt roadway. The other ripped a bloody path into the intestines of the driver.

Bolan aimed the Land Rover at a brick wall, then grabbed the roll bar behind him and vaulted out of the vehicle just before another pair of shotgun pellets smashed into the driver's seat.

He rolled to the ground and whipped three more rounds at the Italian scooter. One nicked the shooter's face, another slammed into the wounded driver, knocking him off the scooter, while the third slug punctured the fragile gas tank. Fuel spurted over the road and onto the sidewalk.

People screamed and tried to run away from the havoc, but the streets were too crowded for anyone to put distance between themselves and the geyser of gasoline.

"Get out of here," Bolan yelled to the terrified pedestrians as sparks ignited the fuel.

As people scattered, the flames whooshed their way back to the scooter tank. The gunner tried to scramble off the overturned Vespa, but was too tangled in the wreckage to move.

Bolan charged forward, hoping to pull him away, but had to stop when the flames reached the ruptured gas tank.

The tank blew with a sharp crackle and a muffled roar. The scooter and its two passengers disappeared behind a huge fireball. Thick black smoke swirled upward from the wreckage.

Flames consumed both men. The shooter spun, screaming in pain, as he tried to extinguish the fire covering his body.

Several men tried to smother the flames with their jackets, but the man's shrieks, and the fact that he still held a gun, forced them back. He was totally engulfed.

Chunks of searing metal flew from the scooter. A number drilled through Bolan's shirt and into his back. He succeeded in yanking out several of the larger pieces, but the others were too deeply embedded to remove.

Bolan looked toward the Vespa and saw only twisted pieces of blackened metal. What had once been two young men was now charred human flesh.

A young woman, shock still covering her face, ran to him. "They tried to kill you," she said, as if she thought Bolan didn't know. Then asked, "Are you all right?"

Staggering back to where the Land Rover had stopped, he nodded.

"Perhaps I should call for an ambulance," the woman suggested, looking at the bleeding cuts that covered his face. "You look injured."

In the distance he could hear the loud warbling of police sirens. There was no reason for him to wait for the constables. He didn't know who the two young men were or why they were trying to kill him.

The woman turned back and looked at what was left of the men. Then, catching the scent of charred flesh, she leaned against the wall and vomited.

Bolan patted her on the back, then reached in a pocket and took out one of the wolfhead insignias he carried. Tossing the metal circle at the charred remains, he climbed into the Land Rover and backed it away from the wall that had stopped it.

The bits of metal digging into his back reminded him of shrapnel. He thought of calling the young CIA agent and asking for the name of a trustworthy doctor. But that would have to be delayed until later. He had to find a place to change clothes and keep his appointment with Sonda Mgabe at eight.

The action in this particular mission had been accelerated. And he was the target.

16

A variety of young couples crowded into Cherry's Too. There were more pairs of mixed skin colors in the club than Bolan had seen since he had arrived in South Africa. Certainly more than he had ever expected to see in Afrikaner-dominated Pretoria.

A few couples were on the tiny dance floor, moving independently of one another in rhythm with the sound from the band. Bolan watched them from the doorway for a few moments, then studied the room.

It wasn't hard to spot a BOSS agent. They all seemed to look alike—big and overweight, with the expression of an angry rottweiler on their faces. Nobody in the restaurant fit the description.

Sonda Mgabe sat at a table across the floor. She looked up and nodded.

Bolan walked to her, feeling the stabbing pain of the metal cutting into his body with each move. He picked a chair to sit in where he could face the entrance.

"You look like you were in a battle," she commented, studying the cuts and bruises on his face and neck.

"I was."

"Anyone I know?"

He shook his head. "Even their mothers couldn't recognize them now."

She waited for him to explain. Instead, he picked up a menu. His body felt as if it were on fire. He was starting to feel like a cat who had used up a large percentage of its nine lives.

The words on the menu were beginning to blur. He looked at the young woman and forced his eyes to focus. "What's good to eat?"

"Everything, if you like Greek food," she answered.

Bolan changed the subject. "Do you have the list?"

"I haven't had time to get to it," she apologized.

Bolan didn't tell her he was in possession of her brother's evidence. He had wanted to see whom she thought were the power brokers.

He posed a question. "What do you know about Harry Desmond?"

"He's very rich. He enjoys making contributions to a lot of different groups," she replied vaguely.

Bolan, having studied the reports from Stony Man Farm after he'd settled into his new temporary quarters in Johannesburg, knew a lot about the mining bigwig and his donations.

"Desmond must get a special kick out of backing terrorist operations," he commented. "He's backed so many."

The young woman was evasive. "I wouldn't know. All I know is he paid for Kenny and me to go to college in the United States."

"And made sure that people knew about it. Every newspaper here and in the United States wrote about that."

"We did have to submit to press interviews when we first got to the university and when we came home."

"And you made sure to give Desmond credit for sending you."

"Well, yes," she replied with hesitation. "It was true."

"That's not the only thing that's true about Desmond," Bolan commented. Brognola's file had reported that the mining magnate was a prime source of tips for the Bureau of State Security. "I wouldn't be surprised if Harry Desmond turned out to be how Volksmann found out your brother and I were meeting."

She looked puzzled. Only Kenny, the American and she knew about the secret meeting. And, of course, Dr. Methabane. But he hated the security police even more than she did.

"Only the three of us knew. The raid must have been a coincidence," she insisted. But her voice revealed her uncertainty.

Somebody had to have known. Perhaps someone Kenny had told in his office—someone who had passed the information to the white mining man.

A coldness passed over the young woman's face. Bolan noticed it right away. She opened her large handbag and looked inside.

He could see the glint of metal as light from a ceiling fixture penetrated the interior of her purse.

She was carrying a handgun.

She started to get up. "I've got to go."

The Executioner stopped her.

"Sit down. You're not going anyplace. Killing Volksmann or Desmond won't bring your brother back. Without exposing Desmond as a tool for the secret police, all you'll succeed in doing is making him a martyr."

"I was also thinking about this Major Volksmann."

"You wouldn't get within a hundred feet of him before you were gunned down."

For Bolan, Major Pieter Volksmann was an enigma. According to the report from Brognola, he was a twelfth- or thirteenth-generation Boer. He was also an opportunist, according to Intel, taking payoffs from everybody and banking the money in a numbered Swiss account.

Not only was Volksmann a bigoted cop. He was also a crooked one. A real two-time loser.

Sonda Mgabe was another puzzle Bolan couldn't understand.

The people at Stony Man Farm came up with almost nothing on her that the warrior didn't already know. Her parents had died when she was in her teens. She had one brother and an uncle, who was a constable in Soweto. There were no black marks on her uncle for taking bribes. He was a real straight arrow. Aside from weapons and the martial arts, her interest was in black history. She studied under a doctor in Soweto who lectured on the subject. His name was Abel Methabane.

She seemed to be torn between her fascination with her Zulu heritage, her love for her brother and her loyalty to the new black government. Bolan was sure there was much more to her, but he didn't know what. At least, not yet.

Sonda interrupted his mental review. Her expression revealed her frustration. "So what do I do?"

"Nothing for now. I'll let you know when it's time to get rid of someone."

She looked determined to pursue her targets. Bolan tried to distract her. He pointed to the menu.

"What do you recommend?"

Bolan let her order, then ate a little of the meal in silence. He closed his eyes for a moment, then opened them and saw Sonda staring at him.

The pain from his wounds was starting to bother him. It was getting more difficult to push it to the back of his mind. But nothing would stop him from his mission. What he needed was a couple of aspirins to deaden the aches. He'd buy some later.

He started talking to keep his mind off the queasy feeling that had started to fill his stomach.

"I think the police have the license number of the Land Rover I borrowed from the KwaZulu farm. And," he added, remembering the war it had just survived, "it's going to need some major repairs."

His back felt as if it were on fire. He tried to hide the pain, then noticed Sonda was still studying him.

"So are you," she said. "Have you seen a doctor?"

"No time. And I don't know one."

"I do. We should have you looked at as soon as possible."

Bolan wanted to reject her offer, but the pain was making him nauseous.

"I have a car parked outside."

The waiter brought the check. Bolan dropped enough money onto the table to cover it and still leave a decent tip.

"I'll be fine," he said, getting to his feet. Then he staggered.

Sonda put an arm around his waist and led him outside to her car.

"If anyone I knew saw me lead you out," she commented with a tinge of sarcasm, "they'd wonder what I was doing getting intimate with the enemy."

"Enemy?"

She opened the passenger door and helped him in.

"You're white."

17

Lucas Tsombe had slipped into the Soweto infirmary through a rear door as the elderly doctor finished taping a dressing on a small child.

Looking up at the new arrival, Methabane patted the youngster on the head and sent him on his way.

The Boasters' chieftain was cynical. "How much he pay you, Doc?"

"Nothing. I felt it was my obligation to treat him since it was one of your men who shot him," the man replied quietly.

For a moment Tsombe couldn't find a barbed retort. "Some children got to die before they grow up. That's life."

Methabane shook his head. He had no desire to continue the conversation.

"I reached my distributors. The earliest they can have your merchandise here is two days."

"Not fast enough," the Boasters' head growled.

"Then find another supplier."

Tsombe was about to leave. He opened the back door in anger, then stopped and closed it. Turning he stared at Methabane.

"How much it going to cost me?"

"Only ten percent more than the last shipment."

"That's robbery," Tsombe yelled.

"You'll just pass the increase on to your customers," Methabane reminded him.

The gang leader paced the floor in the infirmary without speaking. Five minutes later, he calmed down.

"Okay. When?"

"Day after tomorrow. Be here at six in the evening," he replied, then added, "With the money."

He stated the amount, and Tsombe was about to protest. Then both of them heard someone knocking at the front door.

"I'll be here, Doc. With the money. Make sure the stuff is here then."

He opened the rear door and left.

BOLAN HAD SLEPT all the way from Pretoria. He had opened his eyes and looked around as they drove through Johannesburg, then closed them again. As Sonda had pulled up to the curb, he forced himself to sit up. The young woman helped him out of her car and led him into the small infirmary.

Two hours later the lights in the infirmary were still on. The occupants of the neighboring homes were sure that Dr. Methabane was treating a patient.

Inside the small treatment room, the elderly black man continued to pluck at the slivers of metal embedded in Bolan's shoulder.

He studied the scars on the warrior's body. "You've been through this before, I suspect."

Bolan didn't comment.

"This will be uncomfortable," the doctor warned. "I urge you to let me inject something to deaden the pain.

"No." It was the second time the elderly doctor had made the offer. Bolan didn't want to take the chance that the man in the long white coat would use something more than a local anesthetic.

Sonda stood in a corner, smoking a cigarette as she watched the procedure.

"He's a doctor, Mr. Belasko. Not your enemy."

Bolan wondered if the doctor hated whites as much as Sonda Mgabe did.

"Where'd you get your medical degree, Doctor?"

Calmly, as he continued poking with a pair of sterile tweezers, the man replied, "At Oxford University." Then added, "A long time ago."

Bolan studied the doctor's face. He guessed the man was at least seventy.

The Executioner kept talking to keep his mind off the pain.

"Have you known Sonda long?"

"This is not the right time to look into my family tree," the woman commented from across the room.

"Since she was a little child. Her parents were friends of mine. When they died, she became like a daughter to me, her brother like a son."

"Let Dr. Methabane concentrate on repairing the damage, Mr. Belasko."

Bolan winced as the doctor plucked a metal chip from his skin. There were at least thirty more to remove, the doctor warned. And a deep gouge, where one of the shotgun loads had carved a groove along the ridge of his left shoulder blade, needed repairing.

"You're going to have to rest," the doctor told him. "And take the antibiotics and the pain capsules I'll give you, as instructed."

"The pills, okay. But there's no time for resting."

"You have a fever. Without allowing your body to heal, you will become delirious."

Finally the doctor was finished. "One last thing," he said as he filled a syringe.

"What's in it?"

"Tetanus vaccine." He stared at the multitude of scars on Bolan's bared upper torso. "I'm sure you've had this before."

Methabane stuck the needle in the upper part of Bolan's left arm, and the Executioner began to feel light-headed.

BOLAN SAT UP and looked around the dark room. Where was he?

A woman spoke to him softly. "The doctor gave you some pills to help you sleep. Do you want one?"

Automatically he shook his head, then he recognized the voice. Sonda Mgabe. What was she doing here?

He felt her hand touch his forehead.

"Good. You're perspiring. The fever must have broken."

She turned on a small light. He could see the room, which seemed to belong to a woman, judging from the way it was furnished.

He looked around for Sonda, then realized she was under the covers next to him.

Wearing a long cotton nightgown, she slipped out from under the thin sheet and moved to his side of the bed. She picked up a small white pill and a glass filled with liquid and handed both to him.

"For the pain."

"Thanks, but no thanks." He pushed her hand away.

She sat on the edge of the bed, next to him.

"You were having a nightmare."

The fog that distorted the objects in the room hadn't yet vanished.

"Sorry if I kept you awake," he apologized.

"For a reporter, you've led an...active life from the sound of things."

He looked around for his clothes, which were neatly folded on a nearby chair. He tried to stand and walk to them, but nearly fell.

Sonda caught him and led him back to the bed.

"You need to rest," she warned.

"I've inconvenienced you enough."

"We can discuss that at a different time."

Exhausted from the effort, Bolan let his head fall back on a pillow.

She suddenly snapped a question at him. "Are you with the United States government?"

"No."

She shook her head. "I would have sworn that it was Jay who had asked you to—" She stopped talking, then got up and moved to her side of the bed. "Even if you were, you wouldn't admit it."

"I'm not CIA, if that's what you're asking."

"Then what are you? You're not a reporter."

"I'm somebody who's sometimes asked to help the good guys get rid of the bad guys." It was vague, he knew, but it was accurate.

Her voice was tinged with anger. "By Jay Preston?"

"No. You sound like you have a personal beef with him."

"Whatever there was between us ended when I came home and saw how much had to be done," she said. Bolan detected a tinge of sadness in her voice.

"That's a shame. I think he really cared for your brother. And for you.

"He passed on your brother's request for assistance. Somebody contacted somebody who contacted me. Until a few days ago I didn't even know Jay Preston existed.

"I don't know who your friend Jay expected to show up. Certainly not somebody like me," he added.

"You make it sound so simple, Mr. Belasko. Or whatever your name is." She paused. "Too simple."

She crawled back under the covers. "It's too early in the morning to do such heavy thinking. We can talk about it when I'm awake." She looked sternly at Bolan and showed him the ignition key she clutched in her hand. "You're going nowhere until then. I have the only vehicle."

She closed her eyes.

18

Later that morning, Bolan returned to the apartment Preston had lent him as a new safehouse. A note had been slipped under the door sometime in the night, and Bolan found it and an ignition key when he opened the door.

"Call your office. The phone is clean," he read aloud.

The signature was the letter *J*—Jay Preston.

A comment scribbled on the bottom stated that the VW microbus parked in the alley was a rental and that he should enjoy, not destroy it.

Bolan smiled at that and picked up the telephone. He got an overseas operator and gave her the first in the series of cutout numbers.

Brognola eventually picked up the telephone, and after a brief greeting asked, "When do you head across the border?"

"In a hour."

"Good luck." The big Fed paused, then continued. "Thanks for sending me a copy of the autopsy report. Smart move spreading copies around to the press. It made the front pages of the *New York Times* and the *Washington Post.*"

"We've got a bigger problem," Bolan reported. "The rally."

"The Man sent me full details. Got any ideas about what to do?"

"Take out the people who want to kill him, and their backers."

"That'll take care of the white terrorists. Just remember the Zulu politicians hate that he outpolled their candidate by a wide margin. It's a matter of tribal pride."

"Do they hate the new president as much as they hate the neofascist white groups? I don't think so."

"How do you plan to work it?" Brognola asked.

"How do politicians get other politicians to cooperate? Give them something they want in exchange," Bolan replied.

"Which is?"

"The new president has already made some smart preliminary moves. He gave cabinet seats to the Inkatha Freedom Party and to some of the major white political groups. Now he should make the point to them that getting some cabinet seats in the new government is just the beginning. That he's willing to listen to their ideas and act on those that make sense for the country."

Brognola was silent for a few moments. "Sounds like a good idea. Bounce it off your Embassy contact. Maybe he can get the ambassador to suggest it to the new president. One question. What are the white neofascists going to be doing while the South African head of state cuddles with the black and more-liberal white groups?"

Bolan thought about the mission in Mozambique.

"I plan to pull a few more important fangs between now and the rally. This country still has too many vipers waiting to strike."

"Stay hard, Striker."

Bolan knew what he meant. Stay alive. He intended to do just that.

THE SMALL, SHABBY TAVERN was almost empty. Even the hard-core drinkers hadn't pulled themselves together from their hangovers to get into their clothes and stagger into the pub for their early-morning hair of the dog.

Kurt Weitlandt pushed his half-empty coffee cup to one side, then leaned across the table so his companion could hear him without his having to raise his voice.

"We've lost a lot of valuable members in the past few days and a warehouse full of arms," Weitlandt, local commandant of the White Wolves, complained. "What are you doing to stop this killing?"

"Our best people are scouring Pretoria for the assassin," Major Volksmann assured him.

"Are you sure that there is only one? There was that meeting notice the police found beside the Ford Anglia our men were driving. The Order of Death has always been jealous that we attract more recruits than them."

The BOSS major changed the subject. "Concentrate on getting enough men over the border to pick up the delivery of weapons and ammunition tonight. That should replace what you lost."

"You promised there would be explosives and grenades, too."

"There will be." Volksmann was getting irritated at the whining. "What happened to that warrior spirit you demonstrated when we taught the kaffirs those lessons in their own townships?"

"Times have changed. In our day we fought to protect our homes and our heritage. We saw what happened in Rhodesia when the white settlers gave up and left everything to the kaffirs.

"Now my men want to know how they will personally benefit. They want guarantees, not glory."

"Keep the kaffirs too terrified to stand up and fight back, and your men will get material rewards *and* glory."

"I'll make sure the recruiters pass that on to the young men we are trying to bring into the organization." Weitlandt shook his head. "Tell me, Major, is the Weerstandsbeweging having the same kind of troubles with its members?"

"Not really," Volksmann lied. He had held a similar meeting with two local leaders of that group the previous night. They were ready to go to war against the other white groups to avenge the attacks on their men and their supplies.

And Jan Gruber, one of the leaders, had wanted the major's personal guarantee that the American responsible for the brutal death of his son would be found and killed. The white-bearded man had become almost violent in his demand that BOSS set everything aside and concentrate on locating the assassin.

The younger Gruber had been one of two men sent to kill Belasko.

It was becoming increasingly difficult to keep the groups focused on their common enemies: the kaffir president and his supporters.

"Right now you need to concentrate on picking up the shipment," Volksmann emphasized. He looked down and studied the notes he had made in a small spiral-bound pad. Then he looked up at the stout man across the table. "How many trucks have you lined up?"

"At least eight. Good solid Mercedes-Benz trucks."

"Good." He wrote the number on his pad. "How many men?"

"At least forty. A dozen of them have already driven up in their own cars to set up the campsite."

Volksmann added the information on his pad.

"They will be adequately armed?"

"Better than adequate. These are my best men. We'll have H&K SMGs, 7.62 mm Galil rifles, a .50-caliber Browning mounted on my personal Land Rover."

"Excellent," the BOSS officer commented. "I don't want the transfer interrupted for any reason."

"If that gang who destroyed our warehouse shows up, we'll fertilize the Mozambique soil with their blood," Weitlandt bragged.

"If anybody shows up who isn't one of us, be sure they aren't able to leave."

Weitlandt smiled, then ran a thick finger across his throat. "One way or another, they're dead," he promised.

The BOSS major smiled back. Things seemed to be getting back on track.

HARRY DESMOND WAS ALSO sharing a breakfast cup of coffee at his estate, just outside Sandton. Sitting on the veranda, surrounded by peaceful flowering gardens and shade trees, his guest, a member of the former government's cabinet, sounded anything but placid.

"This black man thinks he can change everything just because he's president, Harry."

Desmond refused to get upset. The sky was clear, the air crisp instead of humid and the grounds were in full bloom.

"I suppose we'll have to be more tolerant than we've been in the past. It had to happen, Minister. Look at the history of the United States since the 1950s. And they seem to be surviving."

The visitor's rage permeated the still late-summer air. "It's not the same. Remember Zimbabwe when it was Rhodesia. Families like ours, running farms, operating businesses. When the blacks took over, they destroyed those people. They destroyed that country. Savages, Harry. I, for one, am ready to leave this country with my family. You are fortunate that you don't have the burden of worrying about a wife and children."

Desmond had never married. He'd never had a desire to share his wealth and possessions with a woman.

"You can afford to move to any country, Minister," Desmond said softly.

He knew. In exchange for favors, he had been depositing money in a Caribbean bank account for the former government official for many years.

"That's not the point. What we're dealing with are animals! It's up to men like you and me to stop them from doing to our country what they did to Rhodesia."

Desmond's assistant, Arthur, came out of the mansion, carrying a pot of coffee. The two men at the table looked up as the huge blond man filled their cups.

"Emmanuel was busy supervising the people you hired to clean the house, so I volunteered to bring the coffee," Arthur explained.

Desmond beamed as he looked him over. "Handsome suit. Thank you, Arthur."

He watched as his man filled both cups with the steaming brew, then disappeared into the house.

"I imagine you have a suggestion on how to handle the current political problems," Desmond said.

The visitor's voice exploded into a loud outburst of anger. "Arm every white person. Stop the blacks from trying to act like they are equals."

The wealthy mine owner shook his head. "It's too late for that. The whole world is looking at us under a microscope."

The visitor looked at Desmond with envy. "You're lucky, Harry. If your other interests fail, you still have your gold and diamonds." He stamped the stone veranda floor with one of his custom-made shoes. "It must be comforting to know that underneath your own home are your gold mines."

"It is," Desmond admitted, then paused to sip his coffee. "I have a favor to ask," he said casually.

The visitor relaxed. He was on familiar ground.

"It will require some cooperation," Desmond continued.

In the past the former cabinet minister had made certain there were no South African police or military around when shipments of arms were arriving.

"You have it," the visitor promised. "Another shipment of arms?"

Desmond nodded. "Tonight a group from the White Wolves will pick up a shipment. There is a call you will have to make to some of your friends who are still with the government."

He told the visitor where the transfer of military supplies would take place and at what time. "Make sure no one from the Mozambique authorities interferes."

The former minister knew Desmond would pay well for the assistance of the authorities across the border. The visitor lifted the coffee cup to his lips. "Consider it done, Harry. Anything else?"

"Your cooperation may be required again in the near future."

"For what, Harry?"

"There is only one black man popular enough to run South Africa." He stared at his guest. "Agreed?"

The visitor nodded.

"Kill him, and you delay the blacks from taking control of the country for a long time."

The visitor looked stunned.

"What you are suggesting is murder."

Desmond smiled. "If all of our efforts to discredit the black government fail, have you got a better suggestion?"

The visitor became thoughtful. It was obvious he was searching for an alternative. Finally his shoulders sagged. In a harsh whisper, as if he was afraid somebody might be listening, he asked, "How?"

"He'll be at Soccer City next Saturday, addressing a large rally."

The former cabinet official protested. "You can't have a white man kill him. There would be a massive uprising by the blacks. Wholesale slaughter of innocent families."

"But if a black killed him?"

"Who?"

Desmond didn't answer the question. He signaled to the huge bodyguard waiting patiently at the veranda doors.

The large blond man came to the table, and the mining magnate turned to him.

"If we need to eliminate a black, Arthur, could we find someone to do it? It would have to be someone black."

Arthur nodded. He could think of several possibilities, one locally and the rest in nearby countries.

This was no different than some of the missions he had led when he been in the Special Action Forces. Blacks who tried to change the way things had always been were eliminated—often by other blacks hired to carry out the actual killing. Sometimes it meant killing their entire families.

That's what he had explained at the closed-door trial. But the members of the commission who had tried him were too afraid of adverse publicity to condone his actions. If it hadn't been for the fear of the hearing officers that he would expose their participation in similar actions when they had been in the field, he would have been sent to prison. As it was, he had received a dishonorable discharge—and an invitation from Harry Desmond to work for him.

"Yes, sir, we can," Arthur answered.

Automatically he stiffened to attention, then turned and paced back to the doors.

The well-dressed visitor was visibly shaken.

"I don't know, Harry. I've never been involved in anything like—"

Desmond interrupted him. "It's his life or ours."

19

Kurt Weitlandt was nervous. He kept running his fingers over his nearly naked scalp.

The White Wolves' chieftain had been promised that the helicopters would arrive just after midnight, filled with the weapons his men needed.

It was almost one, and the only sounds he heard were the loud chirping of birds and the angry grunting sounds of large animals challenging one another. He knew that large herds of Cape buffalo inhabited the areas around the campsite. Weighing in excess of fifteen hundred pounds, the savage creatures had a reputation for attacking anything that dared invade their territory.

He didn't need interference from some raging buffalo, or from curious Mozambique soldiers. Even though the BOSS officer had assured him nobody would interrupt the delivery, the head of the paramilitary organization knew he wouldn't feel safe until he was back across the border in South Africa. From his experience, bribed soldiers had a habit of getting greedier when they knew it was too late to change plans.

Six uniformed guards were posted along the perimeter of the camp. They were there to protect the three dozen volunteers from intruders, human or animal. Any Mozambique national who entered the compound would be greeted by a hail of bullets.

Weitlandt was too tense to sit by the large common fire with his men. He lifted his 225-pound body and brushed the dirt and twigs from his combat pants. It was time to check whether the guards were in place. They had been ordered to take care of their toilet needs before they took on guard duty.

He began to move along the outer rim of the temporary tent community. A blond youth in a White Wolves uniform that was too big for him snapped the 7.62 mm Galil assault rifle he was carrying into an awkward salute when he saw Weitlandt approach him.

Weitlandt saluted back and stopped.

"Your name is Vander Mend, isn't it?"

"Yes sir. Paul Vander Mend."

Weitlandt had known the boy's father. A good Afrikaner. He'd been killed in a battle four years earlier, when the Wolves had raided a village, searching for black guerrillas.

"This is your first mission?"

"Yes, Commander." The fair-haired youngster was anxious to impress his chief. "But I've been firing my gun at targets every day for more than a month."

"Good. Your father would have been proud of you."

The youth beamed and tightened his grip on his weapon.

Weitlandt started to move to the next guard when he heard the sound of choppers in the sky. As they rapidly grew louder, he yelled to Vander Mend.

"Pass the word to be alert until we get the helicopters unloaded and the weapons into the trucks."

The youth yelled the commander's instructions to the guard fifty yards from him.

The sentry acknowledged the orders and continued to yell the instructions to the next man protecting the campsite.

"Have the men dismantle the tents," Weitlandt ordered his aide. "We've got a long drive ahead of us. I want to be ready to get on the road the minute the trucks are loaded."

The second-in-command, a short, potbellied man in his fifties, acknowledged the instructions and rushed away to order the others to carry them out.

Within minutes men started taking down the canvas shelters and carrying them to the trucks.

Without waiting for orders, the hardmen in the campsite area moved to the edge of the clearing where the helicopters were expected to land.

Weitlandt pushed through the waiting troops and searched for his aide.

"Get the landing lights on," he shouted.

Despite his huge girth, the second-in-command raced to the control box and slipped several switches.

Rows of lights winked to life on both sides of the landing strip.

The sounds of rotor blades became deafening as a pair of Boeing Vertol CH-47C Chinook helicopters hovered over the makeshift field. Their sixty-foot rotors churned the powder-dry dirt on the ground into a minidust storm. The two Lycoming T55-L-11 turboshafts that powered the aircraft had been eased off their cruising speeds of 142 miles per hour.

As gently as feathers the choppers settled onto the ground. The pilots and copilots lowered their turbos to idling, then slid back the doors and jumped out.

Kurt Weitlandt rushed onto the strip to greet them.

He had to yell to make himself heard over the engine noises. "What kept you?"

"A pilot who wanted us to land in Zimbabwe," the lean, sour-faced man in civilian clothes explained in heavily accented English. "He no bother anybody no more."

He turned to his copilot and said something in Spanish.

Weitlandt looked suspicious. He demanded the pilot tell him what he said to the other man.

"To load a fresh missile in case we run into another pilot who thinks he *muy importante* on the way home."

The White Wolves' chieftain didn't know where "home" was for the helicopters or their crews. Not that he cared. He suspected from the accent that the aircraft were based somewhere in Angola. But it didn't matter. All he wanted to do was to unload the cargo, get it into his trucks and get across the border into South Africa.

He turned to his second-in-command.

"Have the men put out the fires, then bring the trucks to the helicopters. I want to be on the road in twenty-five minutes."

The pilot interrupted. "The fuel we ordered. It is here?"

Weitlandt nodded and expanded his instructions. "And have one of the men drive the fuel tanker over here."

BLENDING IN with the shadows, the blacksuited man moved swiftly to where the trucks were parked. Bolan's face, darkened with combat cosmetics, was expressionless.

Slung across his right shoulder was a 9 mm suppressed Uzi. Securely seated in a rig on the opposite side was the 9 mm Beretta 93-R, fitted with a silencer. The .44 Magnum Desert Eagle sat in a waistband holster at the small of his back. His Ka-bar combat knife was secured in a sheath on his left forearm. Its blade had been darkened by combat cosmetics to prevent the reflection from stray light.

Four fragmentation grenades and extra clips for the three weapons were hooked to the webbed combat belt around his waist.

Carrying a zippered canvas bag in his left hand, Mack Bolan was ready for combat.

The two helicopters carrying the arms shipment had arrived at the small field just across the border in Mozambique, as Brognola had reported. He had watched the pair of Chinooks touch down with a twinge of nostalgia.

The heavy-duty transports had carried him and tons of equipment into remote corners of Vietnam.

Dropping as many as forty brave youngsters and their gear into jungle combat in a single trip, then sometimes carrying their bodies out a few days later, the Chinook chopper had become a symbol of fear and hope for many who had ridden them in Vietnam.

Now useless surplus, they had found employment with arms dealers instead of dying with honor on the battlefield.

Bolan planned to give this pair of helicopters noble funerals. Especially since the weapons they were carrying were being delivered to the White Wolves. The white terrorists had been responsible for murdering outspoken blacks whose only crime was that they had refused to condone the actions of the neofascist killers.

The right-wing terrorists hid behind patriotic-sounding slogans, but Bolan knew their true goal was the death of anyone who didn't agree with them. First were the blacks willing to stick their necks out and stand up for equal treatment. White liberals would be next, then the white conservatives who supported the status quo but were unwilling to support the murder of those opposed to it.

There was only one way to deal with the White Wolves—take away their weapons, then their lives.

Bolan began his campaign in complete silence. Easily avoiding the handful of guards posted around the now-dismantled compound, he had hidden and let a tall, uniformed figure pass. Intent on dumping the hastily folded tent he carried into one of the trucks, the guerrilla wasn't as alert as he should have been. Then, sensing an alien presence at the last instant, he whirled. Too late.

Bolan had slid the Ka-bar combat knife from its sheath and rammed the blade under his victim's ribs. Shoving the knife upward until he felt resistance from the man's heart muscle, he twisted the knife, then pulled the blade out and let the lifeless form sink to the ground.

Quickly he pulled the tent and the body behind some bushes, then paused to tear the metal wolf-head symbol from the dead man's collar and dropped it into a pocket.

Looking around to make sure that no one had seen him, the warrior propelled himself under the nearest truck—a fuel tanker.

Opening his canvas bag, he took out a block of plastique and detonater, which he attached to the metal plate under the engine block. Checking the already attached timer, he set it for forty-five minutes. There were eight trucks in the parking area and a pair of Land Rovers. Each of the trucks got the same treatment as the tanker.

Quickly he crawled around a truck and moved to the pair of British-made command vehicles. He could spare only one block of explosive on them. Which one?

His dilemma was solved by the flag displaying a pair of wolves heads, which was mounted on an extended radio antenna on the second of the Land Rovers.

From experience Bolan knew that anyone who commanded a group of fanatics like the White Wolves would flaunt the group's symbol on his personal car.

With the explosive and timer attached and set to detonate, Bolan paused to determine the safest route to where the helicopters were parked.

Because so many men were moving back and forth to transfer the cargo to trucks, he decided to circle the compound and reach the cargo choppers from the other side of the landing area.

Swiftly he moved between the trees, pausing and pressing his body into the shadows when grunting guerrillas came dangerously close.

The landing lights exposed his presence, but there was nothing he could do about that. To cut the power wires would alert the compound that an intruder was present.

He sprinted across the lit beacons and hid behind the second helicopter. He knew where to plant the explosive—behind the pilot's seat. The problem was that too many men were swarming around both helicopters. And he was running out of time.

Moving to the side of the chopper that faced away from the trucks, Bolan saw the copilot sneaking a smoke.

There was only one way to get to the cockpit.

The warrior eased the combat knife into his hand and moved silently to the copilot's back.

Some sense of danger alerted the smoker. He stared into the dark jungle, then began to turn.

Bolan wrapped a hand around the man's mouth and quickly pulled the razor-sharp blade across his throat. Keeping his hand clamped over the dying flyer's mouth to prevent him from one last outcry, the Executioner lowered the body to the ground, dragged it under the helicopter, then sheathed the knife.

Men were climbing in and out of the cargo area in the rear. Bolan slid on his belly into the chopper, slipped the set explosive under the pilot's seat, then slid out of the helicopter and moved to the aircraft in front of it.

He waited until three men dragged a heavy wooden case from the rear of the first helicopter and struggled to carry it to a truck parked nearby.

The two pilots stood near one of the landing lights, talking to a stout man who was apparently in charge of the transfer. The second copilot was missing.

Bolan looked around, then saw the missing man emerging from a distant stand of trees, zipping the fly of his pants as he approached the other three.

Quickly tucking the plastique charge under the pilot's seat, the warrior set the timer, slid out of the aircraft and turned to race across the field. He headed for his own vehicle, parked several hundred yards away from the compound.

"Hey, you," a voice shouted. "What are you doing there?"

The Executioner turned his head. The man who shouted held an H&K SMG in his hands. The soldier hesitated, then started to pull the trigger.

Bolan zigzagged into a broken-field trot, shifting the Uzi from his shoulder to his hands as he ran. He tightened his finger on the trigger and washed the shouting man with 9 mm parabellum rounds before his adversary could unleash the deadly power of his H&K. Even with the suppressor, Bolan was sure the sound of the burst had been heard.

The corpse fell to the ground, watering the dry dust with blood. Pausing for a brief moment, the Executioner dug into one of the pockets of the blacksuit. The torn AWB membership card was still there. He let it drift to the ground near the body, then started his escape.

Men appeared from the parking area, aiming H&K SMGs and Galils in the direction of the gunfire. A hail of slugs tore into the air where Bolan had been standing.

He was no longer there. He had dropped to the ground, still grasping his carryall. A series of side rolls carried him several yards from where he'd last stood.

Bolan could hear men yelling and cursing as they crashed through the brush in search of him. He replaced his empty clip and fired a 3-round warning burst at the sudden movement of a bush. A uniformed body fell on top of the thorns.

A deep voice cursed loudly. "Where did this damned AWB card come from?"

The sounds of men rushing toward him from behind a stand of trees alerted the warrior. He pulled a frag grenade from his belt, armed it and lobbed the bomb in their direction.

A body flew in the air after the missile detonated, and the Executioner could hear the moaning of wounded men.

There was no way he could make it back to his vehicle on foot. Then he spotted the trucks and Land Rovers just ahead of him.

Running toward the command car without the flag, he glanced at the .50-caliber machine gun mounted at its rear, then looked at the dashboard. The keys were still in the ignition.

Tossing another grenade into the woods to slow pursuers, he jumped into the driver's seat of the Land Rover, started the vehicle and tore down the makeshift road to where he had parked the microbus.

In the distance he heard a voice shouting, "In the trucks. After him. Don't let him get away!"

The VW was still there. He skidded the Land Rover to a halt, tossed the key into the thick brush, then changed cars and sped away.

He stopped short of the border-patrol post and pulled off the road. Stashing his weapons into his carryall, he changed clothes and wiped the combat cosmetics from his face and hands with a towel. Then he stood at the side of his vehicle and listened.

Checking his wristwatch, Bolan knew the time had come. He covered his ears with his hands as a series of violent explosions pierced the night. For a brief moment the skies lit up with the intensity of a Walt Disney World fireworks display.

He resumed driving to the border station in Ressano Garcia. It would take a series of honks from the car horn to awaken the Mozambique border guard, if one was actually on duty. No one was around when the Executioner had crossed the border earlier. A short drive would take him to Komatipoort, on the South African side. The South African Defense Force, which was supposed to patrol the border, was too short staffed to have soldiers continuously watching the dirt roads that crossed both sides of the national boundaries.

Bolan knew he'd still have to negotiate small roads in Swaziland until he could connect with the N4 and N1 freeways. But with any luck, he'd be back in Johannesburg before the morning sun rose, ready to continue his mission.

20

As he walked along Commissioner Street, Bolan paused and stretched. The warmth of the morning sun felt good, even to his sleep-deprived body. He wandered into the CNA bookshop in the huge Carlton Centre and bought a copy of Johannesburg's morning newspaper.

He continued his walk until he found the small sidewalk café where Sonda Mgabe had said she'd meet him. There were a number of empty tables. He slid into a chair at one of them and ordered a cup of black coffee from the waiter.

He looked around at the city. Jo'burg, as the locals called it, was just another anonymous and sterile large city, virtually treeless and lacking the sight and smell of fresh grass. Whatever charm it might have once had, had long disappeared to the wrecker's ball.

The central city was a series of canyons created by skyscrapers sheathed in tinted glass. The fifty-story Carlton Centre, with its huge complex of shops peddling a variety of merchandise, dominated the skyline.

There was nothing uniquely South African about the giant city, he decided as he watched the waiter set down his cup of coffee and disappear back inside the small café.

It had already been a long morning. He'd called Jay Preston at the American Embassy to propose the idea he'd mentioned to Brognola.

"It sounds like it might soften the differences between them," Preston had agreed. "I don't have direct contact with their leaders, but the ambassador does. Let me suggest it to him. I think he'll agree."

"Let it be your idea," Bolan suggested.

"Thanks," the young man said, sounding grateful, then added, "I presume that since a shipment of arms was destroyed in Mozambique last night, you're feeling better."

"I'm feeling better," Bolan replied, and hung up before Preston could ask any more questions.

As tired as he was from lack of sleep, Bolan had decided he had to get some answers from Sonda Mgabe. As he waited for her to show up, he sat and studied the lead articles in the paper and let the coffee cool. The front page was crowded with the news of a series of mysterious explosions in Mozambique.

According to the newspaper's reporter, a number of sportsmen were on a hunting trip. A faulty propane stove had triggered a series of explosions that killed most of them—at least that was what the Mozambique authorities had stated.

There was no mention of weapons, ammunition, helicopters or the uniforms the men were wearing when they died. The reporter did comment that a Mozambique spokesman said his government would file a protest with South African authorities for permitting their citizens to carry weapons across the border.

There was a smaller story at the bottom of the page. Some group had broken into an AWB literature shop on Twist Street and had set it afire. A couple who'd been driving by saw a gang of white youths running from the store before it exploded into flames.

The man claimed several of the gang had been wearing the uniforms of the White Wolves organization.

His campaign was starting to get results. Bolan dropped the newspaper on the empty chair next to him, then felt an object pushing against his shoulder. He started to turn when a harsh, accented voice, snarled, "Reach into your pocket and take out your wallet. Hand it over your shoulder slowly."

He had encountered muggers before, but not in so open an area. There was only one way to handle this one.

The Executioner let his Ka-bar knife slip from its forearm sheath into his left hand while he reached into the inside pocket of his jacket with his other hand.

"Take it easy," he said calmly. "You'll get it."

"Come on. Hurry it up."

Bolan let his body fall to the sidewalk as if he had started to faint, then turned swiftly and sliced across the mugger's gun hand with the razor edge of the blade.

Blood spurted from the severed artery above the would-be robber's wrist. Stunned at the sight, the shabbily dressed young black man stared in horror at the wound.

Bolan tore the cheap Spanish-made .32 semiautomatic from the mugger's bleeding hand, then looked at his face. The three parallel scars above his right eye looked self-inflicted.

"You tried to kill me," the shocked crook muttered.

Bolan looked at the street youth's eyes. Dilated.

Drugs.

This was not his war. Not here. Not now.

"Get yourself to a hospital before I finish the job," the Executioner ordered.

Squeezing the severed artery to slow the bleeding, the would-be mugger ran to a waiting ancient Volkswagen Beetle.

As he opened the door, he turned back and yelled, "The Boasters are gonna get you. You don't mess with a Boaster."

Then he got in the car and slammed the door as the driver, an angry-looking black man with a trio of scars above his eye, pulled the multidented car into traffic and raced away.

The file Stony Man Farm had provided him on South African gangs said that members of one of the largest gangs deliberately scarred their faces.

The Boasters were extortionists, thieves, killers, but, most of all, drug pushers.

Bolan decided he didn't need the additional problem of fighting drug dealers. Then he realized a number of pedestrians were staring at him.

One of them, a neatly dressed older man carrying a leather attaché case, approached him. "I saw what happened. That was a brave thing you did. If enough people stood up to these crooks, there wouldn't be as much crime in Johannesburg."

He took Bolan's free hand and shook it. Then he glanced at the still-bloody Ka-bar in the other hand and quickly walked away.

Bolan slid the blade back into its wrist sheath. As he dropped some money on the table to cover the check and a tip, he heard someone behind his back speak.

"Somebody commented that you got rid of one of the vermin that infest this area."

Bolan recognized the voice. Sonda Mgabe. He turned and looked at her.

She was dressed for business in a crisp-looking two-piece suit, and her long hair was braided tightly against her head. In her hand she carried a leather attaché case.

"A minor nuisance." He didn't want to make too much of the incident. He wasn't here to fight the petty street criminals. But at least one crook was out of business.

"You said you needed to ask me some questions," she said, standing patiently at the edge of Bolan's table.

He could feel the disapproving stares from some of the more staid pedestrians. All they could see was that a white man was talking to a black woman as if she was his equal.

Bolan stood. "Let's walk."

The woman saw the newspaper on the chair. She picked it up and held the front page so that Bolan could see the headlines.

"All right. But let me ask you a question first. Did you happen to be in Mozambique last night?"

IN THE LOBBY of the Johannesburg Hospital, just outside the casualty department, the driver of the Volkswagen was yelling into a pay phone.

"You heard me. Then this big guy pulled a knife on Tweaker and cut his wrist. He sounded like an American. You tell Lucas that Big Joseph said we got to get this guy!"

He slammed the receiver on the hook.

Even now he could hear Tsombe order some of the men to search Pretoria Street for the guy.

And kill him.

An exhausted-looking doctor came into the waiting room and looked around. Then he saw the young black man.

"Are you the one who brought in the chap with the cut wrist?"

Big Joseph knew better than give a direct answer. "Why do you ask?"

"The young man is dead," the doctor said. "He lost too much blood before he got here. We don't know how to reach his family and tell them."

Like himself, Tweaker's only family were the Boasters. "I'll tell them, Doc."

MACK BOLAN FELT uncomfortable being the object of admiration. Anything that made people remember his appearance could compromise his mission.

With Sonda struggling to keep up with him, he walked rapidly down Pretoria Street, away from the sidewalk café.

Bolan came right to the point. "Why are you letting your president speak at a large rally?"

"Doesn't your President speak at large rallies?"

He stopped and looked at the display of men's summer clothing in a shop window. Sonda stopped at his side.

"That's different. We don't have people trying to kill him," he answered as he turned and looked at her.

She smiled cynically. "From what I read when I was at university, people are always trying to kill government officials. Your Presidents, Kennedy and Reagan—someone tried to kill each of them. And one succeeded. That's the price politicians pay for standing up for their beliefs. In your country or ours."

The woman made sense, Bolan had to admit to himself. He started walking again, this time at a slower pace.

"What are you doing to protect the president?"

"Everything we can. At the rally he will be surrounded by bodyguards from the time he steps out of his car until the moment he gets in his car and is driven away."

"Will you be one of the bodyguards?"

"Of course. That's my job." She smiled indulgently. "I don't think any of the white terrorist groups would dare try to kill him. If a white man assassinated the president, you would witness an uprising that wouldn't end until thousands of people were killed. The white terrorists know it. And they know they'd be the first to die. They may be fanatics, but they're not suicidal."

"What if it was a black who killed him?"

For the first time he saw a flash of panic cross her face, then quickly vanish. For a moment she looked like a little girl who'd been caught with her finger in the birthday cake.

"No black would," she said, recovering quickly.

"How about someone from the Inkatha Freedom Party? From what I've heard, they're still desperate to get someone from their party into the top job. It wouldn't be the first time a black killed another black."

She sounded annoyed. "You're talking about the street toughs in the townships killing one another, like the Boasters or the Black Cats." Her voice became harder. "Zulus aren't murderers. They may disagree with the philosophies of the new president, but they don't resort to murder to make a point."

Bolan remembered some of the news stories before the election about the battles in the black townships. Inkatha supporters killing ANC supporters, and vice versa.

"I understand the president gave the Zulus a number of key cabinet posts. Doesn't that satisfy their need to have a voice in how South Africa will change in the future?"

The young woman's eyes glistened for a moment, then became expressionless.

"Token gestures. He hasn't listened to their suggestions," she replied coldly.

"Maybe they haven't made any yet. Maybe they're thinking the way you are."

"Well, if they did he would ignore them. To the new president these men are just stupid Zulu warriors."

"Don't be too sure. In countries like Israel and Italy, for example, the only way a government can function is by setting up coalitions with other parties."

She sounded skeptical. "Who will convince the president to solicit ideas from the Zulu cabinet members?"

"I think somebody already has."

The woman looked puzzled. "Who?"

Bolan didn't answer. He changed the subject. "Can you get me a pass to stand near the president?"

"As a reporter?"

"As somebody who wants to make sure he isn't assassinated by some psychopath who hates blacks."

For a moment her face reflected her doubts. Then suddenly she looked at the small gold watch on her wrist.

"I'll see what I can do," she promised. "I'm late for a meeting at the office, and it's a long drive back."

She started to speak, then changed her mind.

"Try," Bolan said. "I'll call you."

He turned and continued walking down Pretoria Street.

21

Bolan had sensed he was being followed since he parted company with Sonda. It might have just been paranoia, but there was one way to find out.

Look behind him.

Stopping to glance at the native herbal remedies on display in the window of a shop, he saw a pair of gaudily dressed black youths pause behind him.

He slipped into the small store. Row after row of natural medications was on display, while at the counter a handsome young woman in a native beaded costume was getting a prescription from a native doctor filled.

Pretending to study the odd herbs for sale, Bolan checked the Beretta 93-R in his shoulder rig. The clip in it was full, and he had a spare clip in the side pocket of his jacket.

The Desert Eagle was back at the safehouse, but he did have the Ka-bar knife as backup.

He looked around for a back door, but there didn't seem to be one. And the two street thugs who'd been following him each had a hand tucked under a zipper jacket.

There was no way to lose them. Bolan looked out of the shop windows. Pedestrians crowded the streets, enjoying the warm, sunny morning. He didn't want to give the two gang members potential hostages. Having decided on a strategy, he walked to the counter and spoke softly to the clerk and her customer.

"I suggest the two of you leave the shop quickly. By a back door if there is one." He nodded his head at the window. "The two men staring into the shop are going to start shooting any minute."

The heavyset woman behind the counter glanced at the plate glass. "I recognize those two. They've robbed the shop twice in the past. You know, they're Boasters."

"I know."

"Come on," the clerk said to her customer. "We don't have a back door, but there is a small storage area underneath the shop."

As the two women vanished behind a door, the Executioner surveyed the shop. Except for behind the counter, there was no place that could provide him cover.

As he heard the front door open, he eased the Beretta from the rig, setting the selector to burst mode.

The two street soldiers wandered inside and looked around. Bolan turned to face them, the hand that gripped his weapon hidden behind his back.

One of them shouted at Bolan. "Where's the clerk?"

"I don't know," he replied, shrugging.

"I thought you knew everything."

The second tough started to giggle.

"It didn't sound funny to me," the Executioner commented.

The youth who had shouted at Bolan showed him the weapon under his jacket—an Ingram MAC-10 chambered for 9 mm cartridges. "How about this? You think this is funny?"

The second punk continued to giggle. "How about this one?" He showed the warrior the gun under his jacket, another Ingram. "Ephram, do you think he'll laugh at this?"

The two had just declared war on him. Bolan brought the Beretta out and loosed a trio of slugs at Ephram.

Two rounds tore through the tough's face, coring his brain. The third severed his vocal cords.

Ephram collapsed to the floor of the shop. His finger, locked against the SMG's trigger, released a stream of lead. Bolan spun to the right and dived for the floor just before the spray of hot metal washed the interior.

His sudden movement surprised Giggles, who tried to realign his gun with Bolan's new position. But before he could get the SMG around, the Executioner had perforated his chest and midsection with a burst of 9 mm parabellum manglers.

As he left the shop, Bolan knew that, like it or not, the Boasters and he were at war.

"THIS IS WAR," Lucas Tsombe shouted when he learned of the deaths of his men. "I want every Boaster out on the street looking for this American." He grew angrier as he shouted, "I want him dead before tomorrow morning!"

The boarded-up single-story dwelling that served as the Boasters' clubhouse was filled with more than thirty gang members. Nobody asked Tsombe to describe the American.

They had seen their leader break the arm of one of them for asking an even simpler question when he was in a bad mood.

He glared at the two dozen young men who kept waiting in case he had further instructions.

"What are you waiting for?" His anger had reached a new peak. "Get out and kill him!"

Quickly the gang members poured out of the dilapidated structure.

IT WAS EVENING. Sonda took her seat before the council of the Zulu Action Front. As before, they met in the living room of Dr. Methabane's inconspicuous house at the edge of Soweto Township. She had contacted the doctor and asked him to call an emergency meeting of the inner circle of the Zulu Action Front.

Now he looked at her and asked, "You have asked for this meeting. Why?"

She reported on what the American had told her about the proposed plan.

The elderly doctor listened, then asked a question. "In your estimation, is this good for the Zulu people?"

"It would get us closer to our goals," she replied.

"We have waited many years to return to leadership," another elderly black man commented.

"We are the largest tribe in South Africa," another reminded her.

There was a murmur of agreement among the ten elderly men who faced Sonda.

"To not agree would make the Zulu people appear petty," she warned.

Her reply earned mumbled disagreement.

"You said it would be bad for us to refuse to cooperate," Dr. Methabane said, looking at the young woman. "But there is another solution."

The room became quiet. The elderly doctor was held in awe by the others.

"If the president was dead, the only choice would be between the whites and the Inkatha. The Zulus were destined to rule this country." He didn't add that he expected to be one of those who would rule behind the scenes.

Momentary silence greeted his comment. Then a surge of soft-spoken agreements followed.

"The American you treated will try to protect him," she warned.

"Then he must also die." Methabane looked at the others in the room. Each man nodded in agreement.

Sonda felt a sadness she couldn't explain. It wasn't that the American represented a personal future for her. She had already forgone that when she told Jay Preston that she had other goals than sharing her life with him. Perhaps it was that the big American represented something she had rarely experienced before—a clear sense of right and wrong, and a willingness to risk his life for his beliefs.

She felt a foreboding as she asked, "Who will do this?"

"You have been trained for such a moment."

The doctor was right. All of her adult life, she had been preparing. What was the line Dr. Methabane used to quote? She remembered: "The enemy of my people is my enemy."

It had become more than a clever phrase.

There was an emptiness which at first she thought was fear. No, she realized. It wasn't that she was afraid. For some reason she couldn't explain, what she was expected to do felt wrong.

She would have to kill the American, too. He had saved her brother's reputation and fought against the white bigots. But there was no possibility he would let anyone kill the new president, not even Sonda.

The doctor turned back to her. "That is our decision."

Without a word or show of emotion, she stood and left the room.

22

Lambert's Bay was a grim, dirty fishing port. Not many miles to the south was a series of coastal holiday villages that catered to the tourist visiting the South African west coast.

But not Lambert's Bay. The town itself smelled of dead fish. The dozens of fish-processing plants that lined the waterfront reeked of the odor.

Bolan had been on the Atlantic Ocean side of the Cape Province before. It was a beautiful, relaxed part of South Africa, except for the black townships, which, like elsewhere in the country, were overcrowded with starving blacks and coloreds sharing one thing in common—the desperation and isolation they felt.

Jay Preston's call that afternoon about a shipload of weapons destined for a branch of the AWB in Cape Town had grabbed Bolan's attention. This was an opportunity to plant some more distrust among people who didn't have much trust anyway, and to destroy a supply of killing machines.

Preston had insisted on going along. Wearing a field camouflage outfit, the young CIA operative had picked him up in his car and driven to a private airstrip where a small Learjet waited. The pilot, a graying veteran of secret missions, judging from his appearance and attitude, got them airborne as soon as they boarded.

"How long?" Bolan asked the taciturn sky jockey.

The pilot glanced without much interest at the warrior's outfit—a combat blacksuit and camouflage makeup. It seemed as if he'd seen it all before. "Till we get there? Just under three hours if no one asks us to land so they can check our credentials."

Bolan turned to the young Agency field man. "Do we have credentials?"

"Not exactly. I didn't think I could get clearance from Langley for this trip."

Bolan shook his head. "Brief me."

"We got a tip that an arms dealer was bringing in a fishing trawler tonight, loaded with weapons, ammo and explosives. According to the source, the shipment was worth three million dollars, American. The AWB is supposed to pick up the load in the middle of the night."

"That's a lot of hardware."

"That's what I thought," Preston replied. "So I called you."

"And decided to tag along." He studied the sincere-looking young man. "Ever been out on a mission?"

"I had a lot of time on the range in Langley."

Bolan had seen the mock battlefields the CIA had set up at its Virginia headquarters. They hadn't left anything to chance. Trainees had to go through a variety of situations to get them used to what covert warfare was like.

"They don't use live ammo in Langley," Bolan warned.

"They do in Iraq," Preston replied, then added, "I spent four months on the front lines."

Bolan felt a little better about having Preston tag along. "What kind of hardware are you carrying?"

Preston unzipped the long canvas bag he'd brought with him. A .45 Colt Commander in a rigid holster sat on top of a 5.56 mm Colt Commando submachine gun with a 30-round clip. Spare clips for both weapons were stacked in the bag, as were a half-dozen frag grenades.

"Good choices," Bolan commented. "You're missing something important."

The CIA man looked puzzled.

"If we're going to sink that fishload of hardware, we're going to need explosives."

Preston showed his embarrassment.

"Don't sweat it," the Executioner said as he opened the bag he had carried onto the jet.

He handed the young field agent six plastic-explosive packets, fitted with detonators and timers.

"People who want to stay alive are prepared for anything." He tucked the explosives inside Preston's bag. "It'll take both of us to sink the trawler."

Then he remembered something and checked in the pocket of his blacksuit. The metal White Wolves insignia was there. He took it out and glanced at the metallic circle.

Preston stared at the object in Bolan's hand. "What's it for?"

"To get a lot of people mad at each other," he replied, and put it back in his pocket.

A BATTERED VAN was waiting for them at the landing strip a few miles east of the waterfront. The driver, a neatly dressed black man, waved to Preston and got out to help them load their bags.

The young agent didn't bother introducing the two men.

In response to Bolan's questioning glance, Preston explained, "He works part-time for us."

Grabbing the field agent's carryall, the driver almost tipped over from its weight. Gamely he reached for Bolan's bag, too.

The Executioner declined the offer, preferring to keep his hardware in his possession until the mission was over.

"We could save some time if we drove through the townships instead of around them," the driver commented.

"Do it," Bolan ordered.

He had seen the black townships of the Cape Province before. Row after row of dilapidated houses sat on grassless plots. Tall light towers covered the area with bright light that interfered with sleeping. The townships looked like prison camps rather than private homes.

Without speaking, Bolan and Preston stared out the van's windows. The few people on the street stared in terror or anger as they drove by.

Bolan turned from his window. "You sure you want to do this?"

The CIA operative nodded.

The Executioner only hoped that the young agent wouldn't freeze when it came his turn to kill. He didn't have the time to carry him through his first death.

As if he read Bolan's mind, Preston commented, "I've had to kill before."

Bolan reviewed his quickly conceived plan of operation. It was based on his years of experience on similar missions. The young man nodded his understanding.

The three men in the van lapsed into silence. There wasn't much more to say or do until they got to their destination.

LAMBERT'S BAY WAS OVERUN with bars. From inside the van they could hear the singing and yelling of men intent on getting drunk. A typical waterfront, Bolan thought.

The driver stopped at a red light and turned to his passengers.

"Just past the village is a string of docks. There's a small motorcraft anchored at the second one. The trawler is called the *Mary Jane*. Panama registry. It is anchored two hundred yards out, far away from the other boats."

The driver stopped the van parallel to a corrugated metal building wall.

"I'll be back in an hour," he said, then added, "but I can't hang around too long. The South African police are always checking this area for smugglers."

The two passengers grabbed their canvas bags and got out of the van. Bolan slung his Uzi over a shoulder and moved quickly to the rickety metal shack that covered the second dock. Preston followed close behind.

As promised, the small motorboat was tied to the dock. Bolan climbed in and set his bag down, then signaled Preston to join him.

Untying the heavy line, Bolan used one of the oars he found in the boat to move them away from the dock. There was no point alerting anybody to their presence.

Fifty yards out, he started the remote-controlled engine. A loud, penetrating noise permeated the area around them.

"It's going to be hard to surprise anyone with this noise," he warned, then turned the motor off.

"I guess we better row," Preston agreed.

Bolan nodded as he picked up the second oar. Slowly the boat moved out into the bay.

In the distance the two men could see the outline of an anchored trawler. A dim light from the captain's cabin meant that some of the crew were still awake or afraid of sleeping in the dark.

Bolan bet on their being awake.

Moving in the water as quietly as they could, the two men approached the trawler, then dropped the boat's small anchor a few feet away from the boat. The vessel was sitting low in the water because of its heavy cargo.

Preston leaned over and whispered in Bolan's ear. "How do we handle this?"

"First we attach the explosives, then we take care of the crew."

Preston opened his duffel bag and took out the explosives the warrior had given him while Bolan raised the anchor and moved the boat to within a foot of the fishing craft. He pointed to a place on the hull barely out of the water. "There," he whispered.

The agent started to reach out with the explosive, but Bolan stopped him.

"Set the timer first," he whispered. "Twenty minutes."

Preston started to apologize, but stopped when Bolan put a finger across his lips.

The pair repeated the procedure five times as Bolan steered the small boat around the trawler hull. The last one was giving Preston trouble, and Bolan reached out to help him.

Their boat banged into the trawler.

"Damn," the Executioner cursed under his breath. "Get your hardware out. We'll be getting company."

Bolan grabbed the 9 mm Uzi and rammed the first of the 30-round clips into the chamber. Preston reached into his canvas duffel bag and pulled out the Colt Commando SMG.

"Some day I'll tell you about not depending on a safety to keep your gun locked," he grunted, then looked up.

Three hard-faced men erupted from the cabin, each armed with an AK-47.

"Bring that searchlight over here," one of them yelled.

A large searchlight began to sweep the waters below.

Bolan snapped the Uzi's fire selector to continuous fire and hosed the deck above him with a burst of 9 mm parabellum slugs.

The light went dark, and from the deck came a grunt rather than a scream as a half-dozen rounds tore a man's neck apart.

Bolan reached for one of the oars and shoved the boat toward the bow. Just behind him, the bay jumped in two dozen places as someone above emptied a magazine.

A rope ladder from the deck hung down into the water.

The warrior reached into the carryall for one of his automatics. Shoving his Beretta 93-R in his waistband, he grabbed spare 9 mm clips, then started to scramble up the ladder.

Preston started to follow.

"Wait here," Bolan ordered in a harsh whisper, then climbed onto the deck.

Two men with swarthy features stared into the water, looking for the intruders. Bolan whistled, and, when they turned, swept his Uzi in a blazing figure eight that ruined the crewmen's chests.

Bolan forward rolled on the deck just as a heavyset man wearing a sweat-stained captain's cap rushed out of the cabin. Slugs from the Galil sniper rifle in the man's hands ripped a series of holes into the deck. The warrior knew he couldn't turn fast enough to avoid the next wave of lead from the Israeli-made weapon.

A triple burst exploded behind him. The fat man dropped the weapon and stared past the Executioner with glazed eyes, then crumpled to the deck.

Bolan turned his head. Jay Preston was holding the Colt Commando SMG in his hands.

"Not as much recoil as I expected," he commented.

The Executioner scrambled to his feet. "We can talk about that later. Let's get out of here!"

They scrambled down the rope ladder, and Preston started the engine.

Looking at Bolan, he asked, "Does it matter if anyone hears us?"

"Get this thing up to top speed right away."

The Langley field representative followed orders and raced the motorboat back to the dock. As they climbed onto the wooden platform, the force of the explosion out in the bay shoved the two men forward. A shower of exploding ammo and grenades hurtled into the sky and tore the trawler apart.

Struggling to maintain his balance, Preston asked, "What the hell were they carrying on that boat?"

Bolan dropped the White Wolves insignia on the dock as a souvenir for the police, then turned to the serious-faced young man.

"It doesn't matter. Nobody's going to get the chance to use it on innocents," Bolan replied.

23

Reggie Mgabe hated patrolling this section of Soweto, especially at dawn. But he had been assigned to the overnight shift. A few more hours and he could go home.

Almost all of the shops were boarded shut, as were a number of the shacks that had once housed families.

The stench of poverty permeated the area. It was a foul odor he had smelled too often as he covered his beat.

Something caught his eye. A group of young men crowded into the doorway of a shuttered shop. The police constable pulled his vehicle over to the curb to check them out.

Huddled together, they seemed to be passing something between them. The police officer could see money exchanging hands. Two of the men had parallel scars above their right eyes. Boasters.

The constable took the precaution of calling in his location to the police dispatcher before he got out of his car. As he moved toward the group, he eased the 9 mm Glock 17 pistol from its holster.

Fifteen years of service had taught him to be cautious, not heroic. Too many officers had died on duty trying to win medals. All he wanted was to stay alive long enough to start spending his pension. He paused ten feet from the group and asked, "What's going on, chaps?"

The group of young blacks stared at the intruder and quickly scattered in different directions.

Mgabe aimed his weapon at the last two.

"Hold it there," he ordered. "Hands in the air."

Nervously the two youths raised their hands.

"I've seen you two before," he commented. "You're Boasters."

He could see one of them holding a plastic bag filled with pills. "Drop it," he ordered in a hard tone.

The bag fell to the ground, and pills scattered on the sidewalk.

From behind, he heard a car pull up to the curb. A voice called out.

"Need any help, Officer?"

Mgabe glanced over his shoulder. He was surprised to see Dr. Methabane sitting in the rear of a new Mercedes-Benz. His eyes darted to the man sitting next to the doctor. Lucas Tsombe. He looked confused when the Boasters' boss poked a Street Sweeper out his open window.

With the look of surprise frozen on his face for eternity, Mgabe felt the first of the shotgun loads tear into his body. Almost severed at the waist, the dead constable fell to the ground.

Tsombe looked across the sidewalk to the doorway, ignoring the police officer's body.

"Pick up those damned pills and let's get out of here," he told the two gang members. Then he turned to the aged medical man.

Methabane didn't look disturbed by the killing. "How much did you say you were willing to pay for the shipment?"

"The best I can do is forty thousand rand," the Boasters' leader replied.

"Perhaps we can trade," the Zulu Action Front head suggested. He outlined his proposition. Drugs for the killing of the president.

"It better be a lot of drugs. That's big-league."

"Do you have someone who can do it?"

Tsombe sneered. "Me. This won't be the first time I've done somebody important."

Methabane privately mourned the loss of income for his private retirement fund. But sometimes, he decided, duty came before profit. And he was starting to sense that he couldn't depend on Sonda Mgabe's total loyalty.

IT WAS STILL DAWN when Bolan dragged the canvas bag into the safehouse and stowed it in a closet. Then he went to the telephone and called Sonda Mgabe at her home. She sounded guarded when she answered.

"I was wondering about the press pass," he said.

"I'm still working on it."

"Thanks. Did you get a chance to mention the coalition plan?"

There was a brief hesitation, then she answered, "I felt out a number of people."

Something was wrong. Bolan could sense it.

"What did they think?"

Her voice sounded deliberately vague. "I'll tell you about it the next time I see you in person."

"When will that be?"

There was a clicking sound through the telephone. Somebody was trying to reach the young woman.

"Please hold," she said.

As he waited, he wondered why she had sounded so remote. Before he could give it any more thought, she returned.

Her voice was flat. "That was the police on the phone," she explained, sounding confused. "I have to go." Then, as if she suddenly remembered what he had asked her, added, "I'll leave a message with Jay Preston about getting together."

Before he could ask her what the police wanted, she hung up.

BOLAN SAT at the small table in the safehouse and made notes on a pad. Volksmann would try to kill the president at the rally. What he wasn't certain of was whether the major would do it personally or have somebody else make the attempt.

There was something wrong with the logic. As the black woman had commented, a white man killing the black president would start a reaction among the black population that no sane person wanted.

Logically only a black shooter made sense. But who?

It had to be a professional, someone who didn't take sides.

He'd call Brognola and ask him to check out the internationally known black hired guns. If they were all accounted for, there was only one shooter left, and he was local.

Lucas Tsombe.

According to the local CIA operative, the gang leader had a reputation as a top marksman and had a history of killing for money. Only someone like Tsombe would put money first and the future of his people second.

Bolan had less than three days to find and stop him.

PRESTON HAD TAKEN a quick shower when he got back from the small airport, then threw on an Embassy-style ensemble. He had a breakfast appointment with one of his contacts.

"The Order of Death just increased their weapons inventory," the free-lance informant said.

Preston knew about the Order of Death guerrillas. They killed anyone black without needing a reason.

"There's another place, a dress factory on the edge of Tembisa Township, worth checking out." He handed the CIA agent a slip of paper with both addresses. Then he leaned back in his chair. He looked as if he had just discovered a new gold mine.

"I hope you got a bonus for me. I've got some really powerful information," he said with a gleam in his eyes.

He started talking.

Preston was stunned when his informant finished his report thirty minutes later. He set down his coffee cup and stared at the skinny black man.

"You're sure you got it straight?"

"Absolutely."

Breakfast at the small café down the street from the Embassy had suddenly become inedible. But he had to believe the man facing him. He'd worked undercover for the Agency for many years and rarely passed along bad information.

"Sonda Mgabe has been ordered to kill the president?"

Something was wrong. He had suspected she was a Zulu militant, but he couldn't picture her as an assassin. At least not against another black.

Preston reminded himself that his informant dealt in rumors, not hard facts. He could be wrong about Sonda.

He realized his contact was staring at him. Recovering quickly, he asked, "Who hired her?"

"Same group what's hiring Lucas Tsombe to do the same thing. Seems like they don't want to miss."

Preston knew Tsombe's reputation. He'd kill anyone, even the black president, for the right price.

"Who bought them?"

"Some think it's a guy named Methabane."

The CIA operative had heard the name before, but wasn't sure in what context. "Know anything about him?"

"He's a doctor in Soweto. Pretty old man."

"Why would he want the president killed? They finally elected a black man for the job."

"Don't know." The informant shrugged. "He's supposed to be active in Zulu affairs. Runs some Zulu terrorist gang. He used to be one of the president's pals. But when the South African police came after him, he skipped the country and ended up in Libya."

Preston was puzzled. "How would he know Tsombe?"

"Some folks say they have a business arrangement."

"Business arrangement?" The Embassy officer was confused.

"The Boasters push drugs," the contact explained. "Supposedly the doctor made connections with drug distributors while he was living out of the country. Word is that he's Tsombe's big supplier."

Preston couldn't control the whistle that came through his lips. Even as he passed the long white envelope filled with American dollars across the table, he wasn't sure what to believe.

The informant glanced inside the envelope. He seemed satisfied.

"Someone else said that a lot of people were also trying to kill some American reporter named Mike Belasko," he added.

"Anyone in particular?"

"I'll let you know if I find out," the contact promised.

Preston knew it was time to get back to his office and make a call. He hoped Belasko was at the Johannesburg apartment.

24

The funeral for Reggie Mgabe took place at four in the afternoon. He had no immediate family except for his niece, Sonda. Everything that happened after the police had called was a blur. She hadn't called anyone, except Dr. Methabane to tell him about the murder. She had just left the office and went directly to the funeral home.

Now she sat near the coffin, dressed in black, and surrounded by uniformed constables from the Soweto Township police. As the police chaplain droned on about life and death and dedication to service, she looked around for any familiar faces. The only person she knew was Dr. Methabane, who sat beside her, holding her hand.

Tears wouldn't come. She had exhausted her supply when they buried Kenny. All she could give the gentle dead man was the admiration she had always had for him, a decent human being trapped in a sea of jackals.

Methabane kept looking around. Finally he stood and whispered he'd be right back. Sonda turned her head and watched as he walked to a large car stopped in the cemetery drive. He leaned into the open car window in the rear and chatted with someone for a moment, then turned and walked back toward her.

The car began to move slowly toward the exit. She caught a glimpse of the man in the back of the car. His face was marked with three scars. She would have sworn it was Lucas Tsombe, or his identical twin.

Why was the doctor talking to him? This wasn't the time to ask. But she would when they were alone.

PIETER VOLKSMANN WAS getting irritated at the countless calls from Jan Gruber. The AWB officer had become obsessed with avenging his son's death.

Just that morning he had called at least five times to ask if the killer had been apprehended. It was as if Gruber thought that BOSS had nothing else to do.

Heavy hammering at his door got Volksmann's attention.

"Enter," he called out.

The short, white-bearded man shoved his way past an apologetic-looking constable and pointed a finger at the Bureau of State Security major.

"The American who killed my son was sent by the kaffirs," he shouted. "If you can't find him, then kill them!"

Volksmann stood and moved to Jan Gruber's side. Putting an arm around his shoulder, the major tried to reassure him.

"We will find the American. I promise you that," he said in a soothing tone of voice.

Gruber pulled away.

"I'll take care of this myself," the bearded man shouted, and ran from the office.

The constable started to apologize to the major.

"No need, Fritz," Volksmann told him. "The man is upset."

After the officer closed the door behind him, the BOSS major sat down and stared at the wall across the room while he considered a more urgent problem than the death of Gruber's son.

He had no one lined up to take care of the new kaffir president. Then Volksmann smiled when he suddenly realized that the logical candidate had just fled from his office. There was nothing he had to do. Gruber was ready.

The only possible interference could come from the American. He was sure the kaffir woman knew where to find him. And his men were scouring the city for her.

He smiled coldly. She'd talk when they found her.

JAY PRESTON HAD SOUNDED surprised and sympathetic when she'd called to tell him about her uncle. He had promised to try to reach Belasko and have him meet her at the small restaurant.

The young Embassy staffer could hear the bitterness in her voice. "Uncle Reggie was a decent man," she had explained. "Somebody emptied a 12-gauge shotgun at him."

"Any clue why?"

"The police found some pills on the ground. Mandrax. It's a tranquilizer made in India that's popular among the drug addicts here. They think he interrupted a drug deal."

"Do they know who was responsible?"

"The major drug dealers in Pretoria and Jo'burg work for the Boasters. The brutal way Uncle Reggie was almost cut in two by slugs..." Her voice broke for a moment. Then she resumed. "Lucas Tsombe is the head of the gang. He likes emptying guns at his victims, especially when their backs are to him."

"Anything I can do?"

"I need to talk to Mike Belasko about him."

"What can a reporter do?"

"Jay, Mike Belasko is a reporter like I am a ballet dancer," she replied bluntly. "Something is going on. I think he should hear it from me."

As the young field agent had explained to Bolan when he reached him, he hadn't found the courage to confront the young woman with the information his informant had provided.

"Her uncle had just been murdered," he explained.

Bolan hadn't bothered replying that the new president probably had family members who would mourn his death if Sonda Mgabe killed him.

SONDA ARRIVED early at the Three Sisters Café, at the corner of Pretoria and Claim streets, in Hillbrow. The parade of oddities that seemed to wander the streets only at night usually fascinated her. But this night she didn't even see them. Her mind was elsewhere.

In a way she was glad the American hadn't shown up yet. She needed time to think. So much had happened in the past few days. So much of what she had believed in was crumbling under her feet.

It had all been so clear once. She was Zulu. It had seemed so natural to believe that if a black was to run South Africa it should be a Zulu.

She had worked toward that goal all of her adult life, ever since her parents had died and Dr. Methabane had become her mentor. Under the tutelage of the specialists he had found, she had learned to fight and to kill blacks, as well as whites. His enemies had become her enemies because he represented the heritage of the Zulus, warriors who were willing to die to protect what was theirs.

Now it was no longer clear. Going to school in the United States had clouded her thinking. Her brief relationship with Jay Preston had added to her confusion.

A white, she reminded herself.

Like the man who called himself Belasko.

He had come to save a country that wasn't even his. He was much more than the reporter he claimed to be. She could see it in the way he fought and talked.

Belasko—or whatever his real name was—was hard, cold and pragmatic. He fought, he destroyed, he killed—but only those who tried to destroy decency and freedom.

She had never met anyone like him. But, she reminded herself, he was white.

Now she had to make a decision. The council had ordered her to kill the new president. Once she wouldn't have questioned its command. Now she wasn't sure.

Cooperation between the Xhosa tribes who dominated the government and the Inkatha Freedom Party of the Zulus seemed like a reasonable and realistic compromise. Peace might finally come to South Africa.

She wasn't naive enough to believe that it would happen overnight.

There were the fanatics in the Pan Africanist Congress who wanted to kill or drive out all whites. They still wandered the streets of the black townships, killing whites at random, even those who supported the black cause. And there were other tiny black splinter groups with narrow goals who made staying alive an accomplishment.

The whites would demand their rights, even those who had worked hard for the election of a black man. And the extremist white organizations, like the AWB and the White Wolves, had already moved their war against blacks and other nonwhites underground.

She had tried to talk the leaders of the Zulu Action Front into giving the concept of cooperation a chance. But they had said no.

Kill the new president? A month ago she would have accepted the challenge without question. Now she wasn't sure.

Even Dr. Methabane had become a puzzle. Why would he even talk to someone like Lucas Tsombe?

Jay Preston had started to hint that he had some information about the doctor she should know. But he had seemed to change his mind and had said he'd discuss it with her another time.

She felt as if she were in a maze and couldn't find which path to take to find freedom. Perhaps Belasko could help her make sense of the confusion.

Sonda realized she had been deep in thought when she was startled to hear an Afrikaans-accented male voice behind her.

"Sonda Mgabe?"

She turned and saw two heavyset men, in ill-fitting casual clothes.

"Yes?"

"You will come with us," one of the men said, grabbing her right arm.

"Why? Has something happened?"

"Don't make a scene," her captor warned.

His partner had a hand under his loose jacket, and Sonda knew he was gripping a gun.

A waiter, young with dark hair that hung to his shoulders, started to walk to her table. She stopped him.

"It's all right. BOSS wants to ask me some questions. Tell my friend I'll call later."

She got to her feet and shrugged off the hand that held her arm.

"I don't need help, thank you," she snapped.

The waiter watched the two men and the woman leave. He saw her handbag on the floor and started to run after her, then stopped. He wanted nothing to do with BOSS.

IT WAS EVENING before Mack Bolan got around to checking out the tip from Jay Preston about the arms hidden in the run-down Johannesburg auto-storage garage. The neighborhood was filled with small factories and warehouses. Looking inside, through a dirt-streaked window of the garage, he had seen no signs of people. Yet a half-dozen trucks and cars were parked behind the building.

The CIA man had called earlier to alert him that a lot of people were looking to find and kill him. He couldn't bring himself to name Sonda Mgabe as one of them.

Bolan accepted the death threats as a part of the job.

"So what else is new?"

His blasé attitude seemed to have a calming effect on the young man. Preston recovered enough to pass on the information that behind a false wall in the auto-storage building was a cache of sophisticated weapons.

According to the Embassy man, Denny's Automotive Storage was a front for the Order of Death group, whose members were committed to raiding black townships and leaving the bodies of men, women and children lying in the streets.

Bolan slipped into the building after picking the lock on a side door.

He wore his combat blacksuit to make himself less visible to anyone he might encounter. Over his shoulder was the suppressed Uzi loaded with a 30-round clip of soft-nose 9 mm parabellum rounds. At his waist was his silenced Beretta 93-R, and in a rigid leather holster worn on his belt was the .44 Magnum Desert Eagle.

Preston had offered to join him, but he replied that one man could do a better job than two.

He checked his wristwatch. He was on a tight schedule. Sonda Mgabe was expecting him at eight.

The garage was empty, not one vehicle inside to justify the claim of the large sign hanging over the entrance that this was where Jo'burg residents stored their automobiles.

Bolan could hear the muffled sounds of conversation. He moved quietly to a door that he took to be the office. Beretta in hand, he eased the door open an inch and looked inside.

Empty.

But the muffled sounds were louder.

Slipping into the office, he searched for another door. There had to be one for the racist thugs to get into the space behind the false wall.

A soft, creaking sound caught his attention. Quickly he flattened himself against a wall. The Beretta in his hand was set on automatic fire.

A section of wall in the office began to turn inward on hidden hinges. A large man with the build of a heavyweight fighter carried a Galil sniper rifle through the opening.

Apparently desperate for relief, he started to pull down the zipper on his camouflage pants as he rushed toward a small bathroom.

Bolan waited until the armed man moved past him, then wrapped a forearm around his neck. Struggling to free himself, the man twisted and turned.

The Executioner increased the pressure on the man's windpipe until finally the guy was limp. Stuffing a dirty rag into his mouth, Bolan pulled the unconscious soldier to a desk and shoved him under it.

Moving to the edge of the wall opening, the warrior studied the hidden room. Two dozen uniformed men sat in front of a large cache of military hardware.

Ten cases of assault rifles had come from China, and almost as many crates of automatic pistols from Germany. Two tall stacks of crates were labeled Ammunition. And another forty cases contained a variety of explosives.

The centerpiece of the inventory caught the warrior's eye: a .50 caliber Barrett Light 50 Model 82A1 mounted on a bipod. The thirty-two-pound machine gun was too heavy for one man to carry. He wondered what kind of vehicle they were planning to use as a mount.

A coughing sound behind him made Bolan turn quickly. The unconscious man was beginning to move. The Executioner helped him to his feet and yanked the rag from his mouth.

The groggy soldier muttered, "What is—"

Then he stopped when Bolan put the Beretta against his nostrils.

"Move," the warrior ordered in a whisper.

The dazed man led the way into the empty storage area and out the side door. The VW microbus was parked against a side wall of the garage.

The captive started to ask a question. Bolan slammed his handgun against the man's temple. As he collapsed, the Executioner looked down and commented, "You'll thank me for this later, when you realize you're still alive."

He shoved the still form into the back of the VW and pulled out a canvas carryall that was loaded with battle gear.

Bolan returned the Beretta to its holster. Then, grabbing a dozen packets of plastic explosive, he made a circle of the building, attaching a packet to the walls at hundred-foot intervals.

Quickly he moved around the building again to make sure the timers were set for twenty minutes.

Returning to the microbus, he checked to make sure the prisoner was still unconscious. Then he emptied the carry-all of the rest of the explosive packets and slipped back into the building.

He had just finished attaching the last of the packets to the wall between the office and the arms storeroom, when he heard an accented voice call out, "Hey, Kloss, where the hell are you?"

Bolan unleathered his Beretta as a short, extremely stout man in his late forties stepped through the opening into the office.

The Executioner held the gun against the man's neck.

"Shh," he whispered.

"Go to hell," the fat man yelled as he stepped back and twisted the AK-47 he was carrying into firing position.

"You first," Bolan replied, and pulled back on the trigger.

A pair of 9 mm parabellum rounds tore apart the fat man's throat. He staggered from the impact of the slugs and fell backward into the hidden storeroom, spewing blood and bits of gristle on the floor.

At the sight of the bloodied corpse, the men in the storeroom grabbed the weapons on the floor next to them.

Bolan stepped into the room, his Uzi blazing a continuous stream of burning lead.

Two hardmen fell as the slugs tore across their stomachs, exposing their crimson-colored vital insides. A third gunner pulled hard on the trigger of his AK-47. But the impact of 9 mm assailants from the warrior's Uzi threw him off balance, so the few rounds he fired ripped holes in the acoustical-tile ceiling.

Bolan brought him down with a sustained burst, then grabbed at the canvas belt around his waist for a fragmentation grenade.

He jumped backward into the office as the armed hand bomb landed in the middle of eight men. The impact of the explosion nearly burst his eardrums.

Jumping to his feet, the warrior ejected the spent clip and slammed a full magazine into the Uzi.

Hardmen saturated with fragments of the grenade rushed into the office. Like furious wasps, they attacked in every direction, unleashing an awesome volume of lead across the length and width of the room.

Bolan had anticipated the move and had flattened himself against the wall that hid the door to the storeroom.

He waited for the ear-shattering cascade to stop, then stepped out in front of the attackers and pointed the squat weapon at them.

One man spun as several rounds ripped open a cavity in his chest. A second was too hasty in responding to the warrior's assault.

Bolan jumped out of the path as soon as he had fired. The projectiles from the Order of Death soldier's automatic dug into a concrete-block wall. The Executioner waited for the attacker to turn back to him, then put him out of his misery with a short burst that shattered the man's sternum.

As best he could count, he had twenty rounds left in the Uzi magazine. And more than two dozen men to bring down.

Grabbing a second frag grenade from his web belt, he pitched it at the wave of men trying to fire at him. Then he ducked behind the metal desk and pressed his face into the floor.

He could hear screams as the bomb exploded and the sounds of moaning from a handful of dying men.

Glancing over the top of the desk, he could see that the floor between him and the weapons-storage room was littered with body parts of men who, less than a hour earlier, were planning the death of black and mixed-color innocents.

Bolan checked his wristwatch. Six minutes remained before the explosives reduced the building to rubble.

He walked through the garage and out the side door. He pulled the still-unconscious thug from the VW and shoved him behind a concrete-block wall.

"You'll never know just how much luck you had tonight," Bolan told the sleeping soldier as he dropped a metallic wolf-head symbol of the White Wolves in the man's palm.

Then he stripped off the blacksuit and slipped into a lightweight pair of slacks and a loose-fitting sport shirt.

He picked up the light-colored jacket neatly folded on the passenger seat and put it on to cover his handguns.

He glanced at his wristwatch again. He had fifteen minutes to make it to the small coffeehouse where he was supposed to meet Sonda Mgabe.

As he drove away, he heard the deep-throated thunder of the plastic explosives as they leveled the building. He stopped briefly to look back at the shattered structure.

It was an appropriate cemetery for the men who had met there to plan the murder of innocent families.

The gift he'd left with the one survivor should raise a lot of questions and suspicions about who might be responsible for what had happened.

At least that was what he had in mind.

BOLAN LOOKED around the Three Sisters Café for Sonda Mgabe. Preston had told him about her uncle. The young woman had been through a lot of grief in the past few days. He had intended to offer her whatever help he could and save any confrontation about what Preston had been told for another time.

Puzzled that she wasn't there, Bolan turned to leave.

A young waiter approached him.

"Are you supposed to meet someone?"

"Yeah," Bolan replied. "A pretty young black woman."

"She was here. Wait a minute, please." The waiter left and returned with Sonda's handbag. "She left this on a chair."

"No message?"

"There wasn't time. Two men from BOSS picked her up."

Bolan turned to leave.

"Be careful. They can get pretty nasty," the waiter warned.

"They're not the only ones," Bolan said coldly, looking back at him.

25

The two fleshy men had been at it for an hour. They had cursed her, yelled at her and accused her of a variety of crimes ranging from prostitution to murder. Finally one of them pulled a hand back and slapped her face, full force.

He repeated the question he had asked before. "Where is the American?"

"Which American?"

The second thug pushed the first aside. "You're too gentle," he growled, and swung a rubber-covered truncheon across her face to punctuate the question. He had a permanent smirk on his face, the result of a knife attack that had almost sliced his face into halves.

"You'll talk if we have to strip you naked, you kaffir whore!" he shouted, then grabbed the top of her strapless dress and tore away the front.

"Where is he hiding?"

"Who?"

"The criminal who calls himself Mike Belasko. Where is his hiding place?"

"I don't know," she replied finally.

Her response earned her another truncheon beating.

The two men looked at each other.

"A hard one," the larger of the two agents commented. "Give her the full treatment."

The smirking attacker left the room, returning minutes later with a small cart on which a car battery and jumper cables had been mounted.

"Get her clothes off," he ordered.

Sonda tried to fight off the man, but the handcuffs binding her to the metal chair made it impossible for her to move.

The thug shoved a hand under her brassiere and tore it in two, exposing her breasts. Sonda refused to show emotion.

The smirking man clipped one of the cable ends to her right nipple.

"You'll talk," the second security cop promised. "Either that or you'll die."

The alligator teeth of the battery clip dug into her breast. Closing her eyes, Sonda prayed that the torture would soon be over. She hoped she would die quickly.

The man with the cables poured a cup of water down her chest, then attached the other cable end to her left nipple.

A violent charge of electricity tore through her body. She screamed in pain as she jerked backward, trying to escape the surging bolts of power racing through her.

The hardman repeated the action and she screamed again, then passed out.

The smirking agent stared at the still body. "Is she dead?"

"Not yet. But she soon will wish she was," the other agent replied.

"Wake her up," Smirks ordered. "The major wants the American tonight."

BOLAN REACHED Preston at the American Embassy. He told him that Sonda had been arrested by two BOSS agents. "Where would they take her?"

"Not to the central police station," Preston replied. "Too many visitors from the government. They're trying to keep a low profile." He paused, then added, "Give me your telephone number. I'll call you back in a few minutes."

Bolan read him the number and replaced the receiver on the side hook of the street pay phone. He looked around to make sure he hadn't been followed, but no one seemed to be focusing attention on him.

Somehow he knew that Sonda Mgabe's arrest had to do with him. The two of them had been seen in public together. Now Volksmann's men wanted to use her to catch him.

While he waited, he checked his two handguns. Both had full clips. If he needed anything else, it was in the carryall stored in the safehouse closet.

The telephone rang, and Bolan answered it. Preston was on the other end.

"One of my contacts says that the BOSS organization has a special facility on King George Street. Number 54."

"Thanks."

"I'll meet you there," the young man said.

"No. It's going to get messy."

"I can be in Jo'burg in less than forty-five minutes."

"She could be dead by then," Bolan replied. "I'm going in as soon as I get there."

He jumped into the van and raced toward the apartment.

If Sonda Mgabe was dead, the two agents responsible would pay.

SONDA WAS BEGINNING to show signs of life. The two men kept staring at her seminude body, waiting for her to open her eyes.

"Nice pair for a kaffir whore," the smirking one commented, staring at her breasts.

"And her body isn't too bad looking," the other agreed. "I wouldn't mind having a crack at her."

"After she talks," his companion warned. "The major will peel our skins if we don't find out where the American is hiding."

Sonda's eyelids began to flicker. Slowly she opened them and stared without expression at her two captors.

Smirks held up the cables. "Ready for another visit with our friend?"

His partner started to laugh.

MACK BOLAN PARKED the VW microbus a short distance from the small brick building. The only hint that it wasn't just another run down warehouse were the bars mounted on all the windows.

He reseated the Ka-bar knife in its forearm sheath, then checked the clips in the Beretta and the Desert Eagle. Both were full.

Shoving a handful of spare magazines into a jacket pocket, he grabbed the Uzi and slung it over a shoulder.

He started to get out of the VW, then stopped and rummaged through the carryall on the floor. There were two frag grenades inside. He pocketed both of them and walked to the small building to search for some way to get inside.

The locks on the front door looked formidable. Bolan decided it would take too long to force them open. He moved quietly around the building, looking for another entrance.

There was none, that he could see.

Momentarily stymied, he remembered several other weapons in his carryall. Returning to the van, he reached inside the canvas bag and found them—a glass cutter and an incendiary grenade.

It was risky. Sonda could die in the fire the grenade started. But she would die anyway if he couldn't get to her. Since he couldn't find a way in, maybe he could force the men inside to come out.

Using the cutter, he carved a circle in one of the side windows, then gently pushed at the severed piece. It fell inside with a soft noise.

Pulling the pin on the grenade, he pitched it through the opening and waited. Seconds later, he could see smoke and flames churning up from the floor. Hopefully whoever was inside would also see them.

SMIRKS SNIFFED the air. "You smell that?"

"Yes. What is it?"

"Smells like something is on fire."

One of them opened the interrogation-room door. Hot smoke swirled in, choking both men. Together they slammed the door shut.

"We got to get out of here," Smirks said, panicking.

Ignoring the handcuffed woman, the two men grabbed their jackets and opened the door again.

Flames shot at them through the smoke.

Terrified, they held their breaths and ran through the black fog to the front door. Smirks ripped through his pockets, searching for the key. Finally he found it and felt his way to the lock. The key jammed momentarily, then finally slid into the slot. Tearing the heavy metal door open, the two rushed out in the fresh night air, coughing and gagging.

Bolan was waiting for them. He aimed his Uzi at the chest of the wide hardman.

"The woman. Where is she?"

The interrogator faked toughness. "Who the hell are you?"

"I think you know," the warrior replied coldly. "Where is she?"

The BOSS agent grabbed for the SIG-Sauer P-226 in his waistband holster. A 3-round burst from Bolan's suppressed Uzi tore the thug's chest apart. Blood and bits of tissue preceeded him to the ground.

The smirking agent had taken advantage of the momentary distraction to grab his own P-226. Hastily he snapped off two rounds at Bolan. But the Executioner had shifted position, and the shots crashed into the window of a parked truck.

Aiming his Uzi at Smirks, the warrior repeated the question. "Where is she?"

"Burning, you bastard," the wiry interrogator growled as he pulled the trigger again.

Bolan unleashed a long burst of 9 mm rounds that stitched a ragged pattern across the smirking man's torso. He staggered backward, then collapsed into an untidy heap on the pavement.

The Executioner wasn't sure if any more were still inside. Carefully he moved into the burning building, coughing as the acrid smoke penetrated his lungs. It was hard to see through the blanket of thick smoke.

Finally he saw the outline of a door. Rushing toward it, his Uzi up and ready, he braced himself and kicked it open.

Inside the room Bolan saw a shadowy form carrying a metal chair. The warrior turned his Uzi on the shape, then recognized Jay Preston's face. An unconscious Sonda

Mgabe sat in the chair, handcuffed to it. The CIA operative had thrown his jacket over her to cover her nakedness.

The three of them had to get out of the building before the flames trapped them. Leading the way, Bolan found a passage to the street.

The young Embassy officer set down the chair, then leaned his ear next to the young woman's mouth.

"She's breathing," he said, sounding relieved.

Preston looked at the metal cuffs on Sonda's wrists. Turning to Bolan, he asked, "How do we get them off?"

Bolan knelt and searched through the clothing of one of the BOSS interrogators. He found the object of his search in a jacket pocket.

He stood and walked to where the young CIA staffer had set the chair. "Here's a key," Bolan said as he freed Sonda from her shackles.

26

According to a radio commentator he'd listened to on the drive back to the safehouse apartment, the major hate groups had gotten involved in a war of accusations and violence against one another.

Bolan hadn't focused much attention on the black terrorists, but he heard radio reports that the residents of the townships had begun to defy them. Bullies couldn't survive if their victims joined to drive them out.

As he had told Brognola when he called him a half hour earlier, the tide was slowly turning away from the hate groups and back to the people.

Bolan told the head Fed his mixed feelings about the new president. He admired his courage to appear in public and call for all groups to reconcile. The warrior only wished he didn't make himself such an easy target for assassins.

"I'd like to keep him alive through this rally. Then let his security people and the citizens of South Africa take over and drive the terrorists out."

"You will, Striker," the big Fed had assured him with a tone of confidence. "And so will they."

Bolan knew he had earned the right to sleep. Too tired to pull the covers down, he slipped out of his clothes and dozed off on top of the bed.

JAY PRESTON'S VOICE boomed through the telephone. "Sonda needs to talk to you as soon as possible."

It was three in the morning and Bolan was groggy. "Why?"

"She has some information you need to know about. She won't say what it is until you get here."

"It can't wait until morning?"

"She doesn't think so."

Bolan replaced the receiver and rolled out of bed, wondering about what Sonda had to say to him. It had to be important if she was insisting that she had to speak with him now.

It would take almost an hour to drive to Preston's place in Pretoria. The CIA man and he had taken Sonda there after they'd freed her.

She had wanted the black doctor who'd treated him to examine her, but they couldn't reach him. So Preston had called an American doctor affiliated with the Embassy.

As he left the small apartment building, he studied the street. The road was nearly empty. This was the hunting hour in Jo'burg, and no one, white or black, wanted to be the next victim of angry blacks and whites seeking revenge on anybody they could find.

The rented microbus was parked behind the safehouse building. Bolan slipped in behind the wheel, rolled down the window and started the ignition.

Two young black men came out of the shadows and walked toward him. One, he noticed, was trying to conceal a weapon. The other held a knife.

He waited until they came closer, then asked, "Can I help you?"

The man with the knife disappeared. Bolan assumed he was working his way around to the passenger side of the vehicle. The second stared at the warrior.

Finally he asked, "You believe in this new president?" The ugly smile on his face said he didn't much care.

"I'm just visiting from the United States," Bolan replied calmly.

"We think all the whites ought to go back to where they came from. South Africa should be for Africans. You agree?"

"It's a little late to get into a political discussion," he suggested calmly.

The young black was intent on continuing the conversation. "You ever hear of the Azanian People's Liberation Army?"

Bolan knew that was the name of the terrorist branch of the Pan Africanist Congress, one of the most extreme of the black activist groups. But he had more important things crowding his brain.

"I don't really care."

"How about you getting out of that vehicle with your hands up? Then we can tell you all about it."

The young man flashed the weapon he was hiding. Bolan recognized it immediately as a TEC 9, one of the cheap "grease guns" favored by American teenage gangs.

"Maybe we take your money and your car," the armed man said, sneering.

"Sounds more like you're Boasters than Azanian Liberation Army," Bolan commented as he eased the .44 caliber Desert Eagle from its holster.

The armed man grinned.

Bolan could hear the second would-be assailant trying to ease open the door on the passenger side. He waited until the door swung away before unleashing a .44 caliber round at the intruder. The impact of the big slug drove the man backward and punched him to the ground.

Bolan turned back before the gunner could react and loosed two shots. Both rounds punctured the breastbone and carved a path to the assailant's heart.

The would-be hijacker's veins kept spurting fountains of blood as he fell face first to the ground.

Bolan glanced at the two bodies. He didn't know if they really were members of the Pan Africanist Congress. It didn't matter. He dug into his carryall and found what he wanted—the Zulu Action Front shoulder patch, showing a warrior holding a spear.

He let it fall to the ground near the corpse of the thug with the SMG.

Bolan put the Volkswagen in gear and drove down the street before a local police constable could show up and delay him with endless questions.

PRESTON OPENED THE DOOR slightly. He saw it was Bolan and opened it wide. The young CIA agent led the way into the bedroom.

The warrior looked at the young woman under the bedcovers. Her face and neck were covered with deep bruises. She was wearing one of Preston's business shirts.

"You should be sleeping," he told Sonda. "Anything you have to say could have waited until tomorrow."

She shook her head. "You saved my life. I think they were planning to kill me like they killed Kenny. Thank you."

"Anytime," he replied.

"I have something to tell you." He could see her shiver with nervousness.

The warrior pulled up a small chair and sat near the bed.

"The president and you are supposed to die," she said, trying to sound calm.

"Why?"

"The president because if he succeeds, it would interfere with other plans."

"And me?"

"Because you would do everything you could to stop his death."

Bolan thought he knew the answer to his next question. But he asked it anyway.

"Who was supposed to kill us?"

Sonda took a deep breath. "Me," she replied. "I've been trained for such an assignment since I was sixteen."

Preston looked stunned. "Who would teach a young girl to murder?"

She looked past Bolan at the young agent.

"When you have a cause you've believed in all your life..."

The Executioner jumped in. "Who, not why."

"The Zulu Action Front."

Preston joined the questioning. "Are you a member?"

She nodded. "Since I was a little girl. So was Kenny, until we went to the United States."

She smiled sadly. "You planted doubts in his mind, Jay, with all your talk about the rights of people to have a government of their own choosing. And all the other things you preached.

"Kenny came back confused. He took the job with the African National Congress during the campaign to write speeches while he tried to figure out what he believed. Then he stayed on after the election because he thought he'd found the answers he'd been seeking.

"That's one of the reasons I joined them after the election. To spend more time with Kenny, so the people in the new government couldn't twist his mind."

"The other reason was to be close to the president if you needed to kill him," Bolan added.

"No!" She hesitated. "Maybe that is why the council of the Front agreed that I could work for them. But I wanted to find out something about these people."

"These people?" Preston sounded angry. "These people are blacks and colored people and whites who want the same things you must want. A chance for a decent future."

Bolan held up a hand to stop Preston. "Who runs the Zulu Action Front?"

She didn't answer him.

The American Embassy officer joined in the interrogation. "Dr. Methabane?"

She turned her head away without saying anything.

Bolan stood to leave.

Sonda looked up at him and said, "These are sincere people who believe in their cause."

Bolan walked to the doorway, stopped and turned back. "Then they probably will be willing to die for it," he replied, and left.

27

Bolan had hardly slept. His mind kept replaying the conversation with Sonda. Finally, as light filtered through the drawn shade that covered the bedroom window, he picked up the phone.

He dialed Jay Preston's home number. Perhaps Sonda had told Preston something else after he left. The telephone kept ringing for several minutes. Finally he hung up and tried him at the Embassy, but was told by his secretary that the deputy cultural attaché had called in to say he had appointments outside.

Before the secretary could ask if he wanted to leave a message, Bolan hung up.

Right now, Bolan had another place to check, a small factory located in a lonely wooded area on the edge of the black township of Tembisa, northeast of Johannesburg. Supposedly the plant manufactured women's dresses. But according to Preston's informant, the isolated structure housed another enterprise. Weapons.

An Englishman by the name of Nigel Broadbent owned the business. He also sold arms to the smaller hate groups. His biggest customer was a group called the White People's Front, with a reputation for driving through the black townships, firing automatic weapons randomly at anyone they saw outside.

The warrior wondered how Broadbent kept his employees from learning about the weapons cache he had secreted in the factory. From what the CIA operative told him, Broadbent employed only black workers, mostly women.

Bolan would find out soon enough. It was less than an hour's drive to Tembisa.

As he drove down Plein Street, he checked his wristwatch. It was a few minutes before seven. At this early hour the traffic would be light.

The Executioner had originally planned to drive around Johannesburg to prevent inquisitive police from looking into the microbus and recognizing him from the copies of the artist's sketch they'd been given. The longer route would add almost an hour to the journey.

He opted to drive right through the city. If he did get stopped, he was wearing two good reasons for the police to let him go—the Beretta 93-R in his shoulder holster and the .44 caliber Desert Eagle on his belt.

He glanced at the canvas carryall sitting on the car floor next to him. It was filled with gear he considered essential for the planned mission.

The sounds of shouting and gunfire made him stop the Volkswagen and stare ahead. More than a hundred white men and women were hitting each other with fists, clubs, even handbags on the sidewalk outside Shell House, where the African National Congress still maintained offices. Men and women, their faces bloodied, fell to the ground, then got up and rushed back into the fray. A number wore the uniforms of various neofascist organizations.

Several hundred placards were being trampled by the battlers. Bolan couldn't read what they said, but he could see the hate and fury in the faces of the combatants.

One of the warring mob, a red-bearded young man in an AWB shirt, fired a handgun into the air. Three angry-looking men wearing the metal insignia of the White Wolves knocked him to the ground and wrestled the weapon from his hand. One of them began to beat the fallen man on the head with his own weapon.

Everywhere the warrior saw similar acts of brutality. Only a handful of police were trying in vain to stop the dozens of minibattles. They were overwhelmed by the numbers of combatants and the depth of rage that propelled the mobs to continue the melee.

Ambulances kept arriving, loading as many injured as they could inside and rushing away from the scene.

He wondered what had started the violence.

Newspaper and television cameramen were filming the melee. One of them, a young, bushy-haired man whose camera announced it belonged to the Independent Television Company of Great Britain, was attacked by two large, angry-faced men. They forced him to the sidewalk, then took his camera from him and began to use it as a club on his body.

Bolan was tempted to get out of the microbus and rush to the cameraman's assistance, but a pair of South African policemen shoved through the crowds and starting clubbing the two attackers with nightsticks.

A second cameraman moved close to where Bolan had stopped to get a long view of the melee.

The warrior yelled to him. "What's going on?"

The cameraman finished his filming, then decided to take a brief break. He wandered over and lit a cigarette.

Leaning against the door of Bolan's van, he shook his head.

"I don't know what started it, but we got a tip that a number of the white hate groups were protesting that blacks were allowed to rent space in Shell House," the television man said in a blend of New York and Southern accents.

"Is that what the fight's about?"

"Naw. Somebody from one of the groups accused another group of trying to murder their members. Then a third group got in the middle of the argument by claiming that the other organizations had sent their members to put them out of business. Before anyone knew what was happening, the verbal accusations turned physical."

Bolan heard a series of blaring sounds. He turned his head and saw a dozen police vehicles race to the scene, their lights flashing and their sirens screeching. Twenty uniformed officers, armed with clubs and tear-gas guns, jumped out of the vehicles, then ran to separate the combatants.

"Got to run," the cameraman apologized. "That's the flying squad. The hard boys of the police. Lots more broken bones and blood."

Bolan watched the cameraman rush back to the battle zone, then stared at the pitched miniwar going on in front of him.

He had read and heard about such incidents in newspapers and on radio. But seeing it for himself, he knew the first part of his mission was succeeding. Hate was turning on itself.

Bolan started the Volkswagen van and drove to a nearby corner. It was obvious he couldn't get past the mobs. He'd have to make a turn at the corner and drive through the city on a parallel street.

An official-looking car was parked at the intersection. Its sole occupant, a uniformed police officer, was staring at the bitter combat with an expression of despair on his face.

He looked familiar. As he started his turn, Bolan remembered where he had seen him before—on television, when he'd announced the supposed attempt to blow up the Boer monument.

Bolan was staring at Major Pieter Volksmann of BOSS.

But there was nothing Bolan could do about the major for the time being. Keeping the president alive until he consolidated his support from the people of South Africa was more important than going after another bigot. Turning the corner, he stared into Volkmann's vehicle.

The major turned his head and stared back. Then, too late to do anything about it, Volksmann realized he had just looked at the man he had vowed to kill.

28

Mack Bolan stopped the Volkswagen microbus a short distance from the building he'd been seeking. The sign on the front door announced that this was where Fashion Frocks were made.

The whole outside area had recently been paved. Business had to be good, and Bolan wondered if it was as lucrative in dresses as it was in arms.

He was going to play a role this morning. He checked his appearance in the rearview mirror. He had found a loud tie in a small shop, which he wore with a bright checked shirt. Donning a pair of wraparound sunglasses, Bolan opened the van door and got out. He walked to the front door of Fashion Frocks and opened it.

A woman sat at a plain metal desk near the entrance, reading a stack of files. Rows of sewing machines were lined up behind her, each operated by a woman. A group of men stood at ironing tables at the far end of the large open space, carefully steaming finished garments. A pair of men stood at long tables near them, stacking lengths of fabric, covering them with a cardboard pattern and carefully guiding them through a high-speed cutting tool.

On the surface everything seemed normal.

Bolan had seen similar factories in Hong Kong, Bangkok and Singapore. Desperate men and women worked for slave wages, crammed into unventilated quarters. According to Preston's contact, Broadbent didn't concern himself with how his help survived on what he paid them.

If guns were being stored here, did the workers know about them?

Bolan was sure that if they did, word would have been leaked to one of the black groups by now. But nobody except Preston's source knew of the building's dual purpose, selling dresses and death.

The receptionist lifted her head from the files she was checking and saw Bolan.

"You want to see somebody?"

"Mr. Nigel Broadbent," the Executioner replied quietly.

"He's busy. You got an appointment?"

"No, but I'm sure he'll want to see me after he hears why I'm here."

The warrior had already prepared a cover story. He was a dress buyer from the United States, on a hunting vacation in South Africa. He had heard about Fashion Frocks from a number of retailers he had visited and wanted to find out if he could import their line of dresses for his American customers.

Since American companies were still not doing much business with South African manufacturers, Bolan was sure he'd get the royal treatment from the owner.

The woman looked uninterested. "Who should I tell him is calling?"

"Tell him Larry Lasko, from the fashion-buying office of Lasko and Breyer, in New York City."

She used a public-address system to summon the owner, then answered the telephone on her desk when it rang. She repeated the cover story Bolan had fed her, then hung up.

"He'll be right in," she told him, sounding more pleasant.

Ten minutes later a tall man in his late forties walked through the rear door and almost trotted to the front of the factory. Dressed in jeans and a knit shirt that was too tight for his chest, the man looked more like a truck driver than the owner of a fashion company.

"Mr. Lasko, I'm Nigel Broadbent, managing director of Fashion Frocks," he said in a British accent, pumping Bolan's hand. "We can talk better in my office," he added, leading Bolan to a small room at the rear of the factory.

Broadbent offered Bolan a seat in front of his desk, then sat in the chair behind it.

"How can I help you?"

"Funny thing. I'm here on a hunting vacation. You know, get away from the family and my partner for a few weeks. But I can't help it. I see a dress shop, I've got to go in and look at what they're selling. I see these dresses and ask the sales girl who makes them. She gives me your name and address. And here I am."

Broadbent leaned forward. "What did you have in mind?"

"My partner and I run a very successful buying syndicate for stores all over North America. We're always looking for original ideas. Like the ones you're selling. We'd like to consider carrying your line."

The factory owner grinned. "Thank you."

Keeping the act of a clothing wholesaler, Bolan replied, "Anyway, that's my idea. What do you think?"

Broadbent leaned back and purred. "I like it. We should get together again and work out the details."

"When I get back from this safari I've lined up," the Executioner said, then stopped as if he just remembered something. "Maybe you can suggest where I can get my hands on a decent hunting rifle. The one I brought with me has developed a glitch."

The factory owner stared at him in silence for a few moments, then made a decision.

"Can you afford twelve hundred rand?"

"How much is that in American money?"

Broadbent did some quick calculations. "About five hundred dollars."

Bolan smiled. "No problem."

The other man stood. "Follow me."

The Executioner got up and let the man lead the way to the back of the factory. Rows of women stared at the two men as they passed by.

Broadbent opened the door that led to the outside of the building. Once outside, he reached down and opened the padlock on the bulkhead doors with a key on his chain. He swung open the doors, revealing stairs that led down to a subterranean storage area.

"In here," he said, leading the way.

Cases of weapons lined the walls of the underground storeroom.

"Wait here," Broadbent ordered.

Bolan quickly surveyed the area, memorizing the approximate size and shape of the area. The factory owner returned with a bolt-action 7 mm Remington Magnum Weatherby Vanguard VGX that held three rounds in its fixed magazine. A Weatherby Supreme scope on a Buehler mount was fitted on top of the hunting weapon. The twenty-two-inch barrel fit into a Monte Carlo stock with custom checkering and recoil pad.

He handed the rifle to Bolan. Continuing his pose, the warrior pretended to be awkward about handling the hunting rifle. He had fired the same model before and found it accurate and powerful.

"Looks good," he said. "Got any ammunition?"

"How much?"

"I don't know. Maybe fifty rounds."

Broadbent returned with four large boxes. "No charge for this. It's a little gift from me."

Together they left the basement storeroom and returned to ground level. The factory owner carefully locked the metal doors and led Bolan around the outside of the building to where the microbus was parked.

"No point in letting the help know about this," the dress manufacturer commented.

Bolan carefully counted out five hundred dollars and handed it to the other man. "I'll call you in a week when I get back from the hunting trip."

The Executioner hadn't bothered to mention he would be returning much sooner than that.

IT WAS EVENING when Bolan pulled the Volkswagen up to the factory. All the lights were out, and the front door, when he checked it, was locked.

Slipping the canvas carryall over a shoulder, he worked his way around to the rear of the building.

A pair of metal cutters from his bag severed the hasp that secured the padlock. Swinging open the doors, Bolan waved a lit flashlight in front of him and moved down the metal steps.

Silently he moved through the aisles of the concrete-block enclosure. No one was hidden in the basement. He wasted no time as he started to place explosive packets around the huge room. Setting the timers for thirty minutes, he finished his task in short order and headed back to the steps.

He heard male voices from above and saw the metal doors close. He was trapped.

Playing his flashlight beam along the walls, he looked for a solution. The weapons in his bag were useless, even the fragmentation grenades. Thrown against the metal doors, they would cause more damage in the basement than outside.

He spotted a shoulder-held missile launcher leaning against one of the shelves. He lifted it and checked the load it carried, a 66 mm round with a hollowpoint nose, shaped like a small teacup. The whole unit weighed about five pounds.

He'd never used the weapon against doors, but he knew if it was able to cut through the steel walls of an armored vehicle, it should do at least as well here.

Bolan checked to make sure there was enough distance between the rear block wall of the basement and himself—at least a hundred yards—to prevent the back flash from charring him, then pulled the safety pin. The end caps fell away, and the weapon telescoped another six inches while it armed itself.

Sighting through the eyepiece that moved into position on top of the launcher, Bolan focused on the metal doors at the top of the steps.

He could hear Broadbent's muffled voice on the other side. "Everybody got their guns ready?" Then a pause. "When I open the doors, we kill whoever's down there."

Bolan waited until he saw the doors overhead begin to move, then he pulled the trigger. The missile raced out of the tube at a speed of almost five hundred feet per second and easily punched a hole through the doors.

Bolan dropped the launcher and dived as far as he could to the right of the bulkheads. He could hear the missile exploding with the deafening sound of thunder tearing a huge tree in half. Molten bits of metal from the warhead and flames shot back through the wide hole in the door and scorched the steps. The stench of burnt paint from the concrete-block wall at the rear of the cellar choked him.

He could hear screams as superheated chunks of metal and flame consumed men and weapons. The foul smell of burning flesh rushed down the steps and washed over him.

He waited for the intense heat to dissipate, then lifted his bag and moved gingerly up the still-hot steps.

As he worked his way past blackened bodies and the charred remains of weapons, he checked his watch. Ten minutes were left on the timers downstairs. There was no time to wonder what group the dead represented.

The Executioner moved quickly around the outside of the building and got into the Volkswagen microbus.

He reached into his pocket and took out an AWB cloth patch, then hung his hand out of the opened car window and let the fabric square with the swastikalike emblem float to the ground.

29

They had spent the day together, driving around the outskirts of Johannesburg, barely speaking to each other. There was a coldness between them. The secret Sonda had carried for so many years was no longer a secret, and she wondered what Jay Preston would do.

Evening had arrived, and still there was little communication between them. Glancing at Preston, she saw that he was deep in thought, as if he were trying to decide his next move. Finally he turned to her.

"I want to talk to Dr. Methabane," he said with determination.

"No," she replied firmly.

"You either drive me to his office or I'll go there on my own," he warned.

She surrendered and headed for the doctor's Soweto infirmary.

When she stopped her vehicle near the small house, she turned to Preston. "Let me talk to him first," she pleaded.

He watched as she got out of the car and walked to the door that led to Methabane's medical office. She knocked, and when the door opened she stepped inside.

The Embassy man waited, then decided to get out and look around.

Inside, Sonda spent fifteen minutes trying to explain why she had told Preston about the Zulu Action Front.

"After he and..." She decided not bring up Mike Belasko's name. "After he rescued me and took me to his home, I felt he had a right to know how I felt."

Methabane showed his disappointment. "So you told him about us. About me."

"No," she insisted. "He seemed to know about you from another source."

"This is not good, child. For the sake of the Front, this man must be eliminated."

Sonda looked shocked. "He is an American official. To kill him would bring a major investigation."

The doctor smiled. "No. We will dispose of him in some remote place afterward."

She knew he meant for her to carry out the execution. She looked confused. "There must be another way."

"No. Call me when it is done," he said, then looked at the large clock hanging on the wall. "Now you must leave. I'm expecting somebody in a few minutes."

Feeling trapped, Sonda turned to leave. She heard a door behind her open. Preston stepped into the room. His face was a mask of cold hate. In his right hand, he gripped a .45 ACP Colt Commander.

"Do you dispense a lot of Mandrax to your patients, Doctor?"

He threw a plastic bag filled with brightly colored pills at Methabane.

Sonda looked puzzled. "What's wrong, Jay?"

"The good doctor has fifty cases of Mandrax in the back room. And a large quantity of Dagga, as well as boxes of drugs I can't identify."

The elderly doctor turned to Sonda. "He's lying, child. He is trying to create a rift between us. There are no such quantities in the other room."

Preston pushed the door to the back room wide open. Sonda walked to it. As the Embassy staffer had said, the space was crowded with cases.

She turned to Methabane. "Drugs? Why?"

"You don't understand. We needed funds. This was the only way to raise them quickly."

She looked at him in disgust. Her years of admiration crumbled as she saw a frightened, trapped old man.

Before she could say anything, Methabane began to speak rapidly, his nervousness echoing in his voice.

"I have dedicated my—"

She interrupted him. "Stop. I don't want to hear any more lies," she shouted.

The frail little man looked desperate. "None of us are blameless. Have you told this man about the two people you had to kill?"

Preston had moved to the small desk. He glanced at the calendar, then looked at Methabane.

"What she has to tell me will have to wait." He pointed to the appointment pad. "You have a meeting at six with someone with the initial *T.* Lucas Tsombe, Doctor?"

Methabane shook his head as he slipped a hand into his jacket pocket and withdrew a .25-caliber Beretta Model 950BS-EL with a two inch barrel. He squeezed the trigger, but Preston darted out of the path of the small slug, which dug into the opposite wall.

Before the CIA operative could reply with his Colt, a loud explosion from another gun rang in the small infirmary. Preston turned his head. Sonda pulled the trigger of her Heckler & Koch P-7 M-8 repeatedly as tears ran down her cheeks.

The frail old man collapsed, his mouth frozen in an explanation that only the devil would hear.

Before he could move to her side, Preston heard a car screech to a stop behind the house. Quickly he moved into the back room and opened the rear door. Two men got out of a Mercedes-Benz 500 without turning off the engine. Both cradled MAC-10 SMGs in their arms.

He sensed that Sonda was behind him. She stepped out and stood at his side.

"It's over, Tsombe," she shouted as she began to fire her pistol.

Darting to avoid the slugs from her H&K pistol, Tsombe hastily returned fire, punching holes in the outside wall of the small medical structure.

"For Uncle Reggie," Sonda yelled as she emptied the clip at the scarred man.

The Boasters' chief dived to the ground. Lead carved the air above him and he rolled behind the Mercedes to escape the deadly fire.

Preston joined in the fray, his Colt Commander coughing round after round. One of them tore into the throat of the beefy man who had accompanied Tsombe. Grabbing his shredded neck, the street hood emptied his weapon at Sonda and Preston.

Both of them ducked away from the savage response. Slugs tore into the stucco wall behind them.

Tsombe took advantage of the momentary confusion and shoved himself into his car. Jamming down the gas pedal, he raced away before Sonda or Preston could fire again.

The dying thug tried to clear his throat of the frothy blood that kept gagging him. Preston knelt next to him.

In a soft voice he asked, "Where did your boss go?"

The thug smiled, then his head rolled to one side and eyes glazed.

Sonda and Preston walked back into the building. The blood from Methabane's body had stained the floor a dark red. The young woman stared at it for a long time.

"I spent my entire adult life believing in him," she said sadly. "He taught me so much about my heritage."

She opened a cabinet and took out a white sheet. Kneeling, she covered the old man's corpse with it, then stood and looked at Preston.

"It's all over, isn't it?"

Preston looked confused. "I guess we call the police anonymously and tell them about the drugs," he replied.

"And about me?"

Quickly he made a decision. "The war is over as far as you're concerned."

Sonda thought of Tsombe and Volksmann and the murders of her brother and uncle.

"No, not yet. There are some things I still have to do."

Preston wondered if she meant the assassination of the president. He hoped not. Belasko or he would have to kill her if she did.

THE DEATH of the Soweto doctor was the main topic on the local radio station's news broadcast. Lucas Tsombe, resting on a cot in a rear room of his headquarters, flung a bottle of Castle lager beer against a nearby wall when he heard the story.

The explosion of the bottle as it shattered didn't soften the rage he felt. His main source was gone, and so were the supplies.

He would have gotten them free, just for killing somebody. It had been a sweet deal, if the old man hadn't been killed.

Now he had a problem. Thousands of customers were willing to pay anything for what his men sold, and his inventory was almost gone. He searched for a solution. Break into the Soweto police station and steal the supplies back?

He'd lose too many men, and there was no guarantee that he'd recover the drugs. In frustration he grabbed the Street Sweeper lying on the floor and emptied its circular magazine of shotgun shells into a wall.

Plaster chunks filled the already-stale air with dust. The Boasters' chieftain threw the emptied weapon across the room and sat up. Then he realized he wasn't alone.

He recognized the tall blond man who watched him from the open doorway. Several years earlier, the former Special Action Forces officer had hired him to help his men find the jungle hideout of a group of black activists.

Tsombe glared at him. "What do you want?"

"I've got a business proposition for you," the visitor said coldly.

Tsombe shrugged. "What?"

"We need an expert marksman to kill a man."

"Who?"

The blond man shrugged. "Does it really matter?"

"Yeah. My price is based on how difficult it is."

"Fifty thousand rand."

The Boasters' leader was impressed. "Must be someone important."

"It has to be done on Saturday," the visitor continued as if Tsombe hadn't interrupted him.

Something clicked in the scarred man's head. Methabane had said the new black president was speaking at Soccer City on Saturday. He was certain the visitor was after the same man.

"Anything specific you want to tell me?"

The blond man shook his head. "Just take care of him when he speaks at Soccer City." He reached into a pocket and took out a long envelope, which he tossed to Tsombe. "Here's half the money. The rest will be delivered after he's dead."

Before the Boasters' boss could comment, the blond man left the shop. Tsombe could hear the engine of a car roar as he raced away.

Counting the money, he smiled at how quickly his fortunes had changed. The old man and his supplies were gone, but fresh money had just arrived. He put the money back in the envelope.

Glancing at the envelope, he recognized the company name printed on it. Desmond Mining Syndicate. Really big-time.

Maybe, the man with the triple scars on his face wondered, it was time to handle the assignment, collect the rest of the money and leave the country.

He wondered where his talents would be appreciated. Perhaps a place like Angola.

30

Edgar Mlaba sat at the end of the table and waited until everyone had an opportunity to study his copy of the layout of the Soccer City stadium. As head of security, he wanted to make sure that everything possible was being done to protect the safety of the president.

"Soccer City can hold a hundred and thirty thousand people," the man said in a brusque voice. He ran a hand through his closely cropped gray hair and continued, "As you can see, there is a clear view of where the president will be standing from any place in the stadium. So an assassin can sit anywhere."

Sonda studied the diagram, then raised her hand. Mlaba pointed to her.

"Not unless he doesn't mind being killed," she offered. "The crowds would tear him apart the moment he showed a weapon."

The five other members of the security team nodded in agreement.

"You're right," the security chief agreed. "But there are those kind of psychopaths."

"If someone is willing to die, I don't see how anything could stop him," a young man at the conference table commented.

The security head wore his frustration on his face. "What makes it a serious problem is that the president has made it clear that he will not stand behind a Plexiglas protective shield when he makes his speech. This means that anyone who wants to kill him will have an easy target."

The young man raised his hand. Mlaba pointed to him. "Is there anything we can do to protect him?"

"You and Andrew are new, Paul. The two men you replaced couldn't do anything to protect themselves from the murderers who shot them in cold blood." He took a deep breath, then pushed his chair back and stood. "Let's drive out to Baragwanath Road and take a look at the stadium. We might come up with other factors to consider."

As she got up, Sonda glanced quickly at the two new members of the team. A shiver of guilt raced through her as she remembered the two they had replaced, the two she had been forced to kill.

STILL IN HIS UNDERWEAR, Lucas Tsombe locked the front door before opening the gray composite case. He had invested more than nine thousand rand to acquire the weapon and scope inside. The parts to the target rifle sat neatly in compartments shaped to hold them in place. The twenty-inch barrel fit in a depression at the top of the plastic inner lining. Below it, the AR-15-style composite stock sat snugly in its own recessed area. The Leupold 30 mm M3-10x scope was seated in its own niche.

Assembled, the Stoner SR-25 could throw up to twenty rounds of 168-grain .308 power at a target over a thousand yards away. The weapon had a flat trajectory and could place hollowpoint loads—traveling at twenty-two hundred feet per second—within a two-inch circle.

The single-space trigger had a four-and-a-half-pound pull, making it easy to fire without jerking the rifle. And, like the M-16, the SR-25 could be assembled in minutes.

This was the perfect assassin's weapon. It had distance, power and accuracy. The only problem was escaping after hitting the target.

Tsombe thought he had a solution. The speakers that would carry the target's words to the hundred or so thousand spectators were being installed along the upper level of the stadium. Because of their volume, no one would be sitting near them. But the newspaper stories said that recorded martial music would herald the movement of the new president to the speaker's stand.

The percussion of the recorded drums should easily cover the sound of the rifle as it was fired. And while everyone showed their shock at the assassination, he could make his escape.

He mourned having to leave the weapon behind, but he knew he could always buy a replacement with his fee.

There was no way he could carry in the gun case the next day, as the spectators entered. He would have to take it to the stadium today and find a safe place to store it until it was time to go to work.

He thought of an electrical storage locker on the top level. He had used it before, to store drugs for distribution to customers attending one of the rock concerts in the huge stadium.

Reaching for a pair of jeans, he started to pull them on. It was time to drive to Soccer City.

MACK BOLAN WANDERED through the nearly empty soccer stadium. It was huge, larger than it seemed from the architect's plan he had studied.

Preston had passed the rumor to him that an assassin would make an attempt on the president's life at the rally. And with it, he'd provided the warrior with a photo of Lucas Tsombe, who'd been named as the hired gunman.

Bolan kept looking for likely hiding places. Where would an assassin position himself? Not in the stands. He would be killed by the crowds before a shot could be fired.

The warrior watched the handful of workmen decorating the speaker's stand with multicolored bunting that reflected the main colors of the South African flag.

Other workers were busy installing extra speakers around the upper perimeter of the stadium. According to the schedule he'd obtained, loud martial music would blare from every speaker in the arena as the president entered and took his place on the speaker's platform. They would carry his words to the more than one hundred thousand men, women and children who were expected to show up in the morning.

An enclosed press box faced where the president would be speaking. An assassin could use it as a base, except that the booth would be crowded with television cameramen from around the world.

No, the warrior decided, if an assassin dared make the attempt at tomorrow's rally, it would be from the upper level.

Across the field, he saw Sonda and five conservatively dressed men walk toward the stands. He thought about joining them, then changed his mind. They had their job to do, and he had his.

That they all had the same goal was coincidence. He had no need to socialize. Too many questions he wouldn't answer could hamper his mission. He turned and walked toward an exit.

He'd be back at dawn, at the latest, and he'd be ready.

TSOMBE WAITED behind a flight of stairs and watched the group of men and women cross the field, scanning in every direction. In his hand he carried a large rectangular case.

The group wandered past without noticing him and disappeared down a walkway. The opportunity he had waited for was here.

Quickly he moved up the stairs. A workman, tightening the handrails on a pedestrian incline, looked up at him. Tsombe waved and kept moving.

A meshed wire door barred the final flight of steps from the public. Beyond it, he could hear the hammering of workmen.

He inserted a key into the lock and turned the handle. A long time ago he had paid a guard with free drugs for the keys to the door and to one of the lockers upstairs, which he used to store merchandise.

Tsombe climbed the steps, checking that nobody was watching him. As he reached the top, he saw several teams too busy bolting speakers to metal stanchions to pay attention to him.

Quickly he moved down a narrow passageway until he reached a row of metal lockers. The middle one of the three was the one he had used for storage.

He took another key from his pocket and opened the door. The carrying case and its lethal contents fit neatly inside. He placed the two 20-round clips he'd brought with him on top of the composite container and locked the door.

Turning to leave, he bumped into a workman carrying a heavy circle of speaker wire. The coil fell from the man's arm.

"Watch where you're going," the craftsman grumbled.

"Sorry," Tsombe said, trying to sound meek as he bent to help the man retrieve the wire. Then he turned and quickly walked toward the stairs.

31

Bolan had gone out and purchased the morning newspaper and a container of coffee. He was in the middle of an article about a shoot-out in Soweto Township. Four members of a gang called the Boasters had been killed. The police speculated a rival gang had been responsible, but Bolan knew better. Sonda Mgabe had to have recovered from her interrogation.

The telephone rang and Bolan picked up the handset.

"Have you watched the news?" Jay Preston asked without preamble.

"No, I was reading the paper. Why?"

"Turn to page two," the young agent said.

Bolan did. The headline that covered most of the top of the page reported the murder of a Soweto doctor, a Dr. Methabane, and the discovery of quantities of illegal drugs in his office.

Bolan whistled softly and scanned the story.

Police, responding to an anonymous tip, had searched the doctor's office and found a huge cache of Mandrax and Dagga in a storeroom. They speculated that the doctor had been killed by business associates during a disagreement. According to the story, police were planning to round up and interrogate all known drug dealers.

Bolan asked the obvious question. "Who killed him? Tsombe?"

"Sonda," Preston replied quietly. "I was there."

"Why?"

The CIA operative quickly briefed him.

"What about her mission?"

Preston's voice became flat. "She still believes in the Zulu cause."

Bolan didn't want to kill her, but he was beginning to believe there was no other way to stop her.

"You were invited to a cocktail party tonight," the Langley representative said.

The warrior was surprised. "By whom?"

"Harry Desmond, the mining billionaire. He asked me to invite you to come to the party if I happened to hear from you."

To Bolan, it sounded like a setup. He wasn't sure for what. He was about to decline when he realized it would be a good opportunity to find out why Desmond wanted to meet him.

"What's the occasion?"

"From what I've been told, he has one every year around this time."

"Who else will be there?"

"Mostly diplomats and politicians. Pretty dull bunch. I'm guessing somebody you want to meet will be there, too. Major Pieter Volksmann, of the Bureau of State Security."

Bolan agreed to show up, then asked, "How about Sonda?"

"I'm bringing her as my guest."

He gave the warrior the address and time of the party, then hung up.

Bolan searched through his papers and found Brognola's report on Desmond. Dropping into an easy chair, he studied it again.

DRESSED IN BLACKSUIT and wearing camouflage makeup, the Executioner used the night as cover while he scouted Desmond's complex. Bolan wanted a preview of what he was going to encounter in a few minutes.

The estate was large, at least eight acres. A high brick wall surrounded the property, and strung across the top was electrified barbed wire.

Bolan managed to find a hill behind the estate from which he could see the grounds. Using a pair of night-vision binoculars, he studied the property.

The big house, with its large veranda, sat at the south end of the estate. Next to it were servants' quarters and a garage. The rest of the property consisted of manicured lawns, with large shade trees growing every hundred feet or so.

Six men walked the perimeter, and from the way they carried themselves, Bolan assumed they had spent much of their adult life in the military.

All of them were dressed in lightweight dark suits, cut loose to hide whatever side arms they carried underneath. The black boots they wore were polished to mirror finishes. Their haircuts were short, almost military. Each carried an identical weapon—a Heckler & Koch Model 94 carbine, fitted with a telescoping stock and a 30-round magazine.

The way the guards moved in precise cadence to some unspoken command as they walked their assigned areas reminded him of a military drill team he had seen perform at Fort Bragg. These weren't just bodyguards. These men were trained soldiers.

Brognola's report said Desmond's personal bodyguard was a former Special Action Forces lieutenant. Bolan would guess that the men watching the Desmond estate were under his command.

Formidable enemies, the warrior decided as he searched for possible entrances and exits to the property. There were none, except for the front gate and the tradesmen's entrance.

Desmond or the ex-lieutenant had planned well. Nobody could sneak in or out. Any action Bolan took would have to be out in the open, with the odds being at least six trained combat soldiers against him. Seven, if he included Desmond's personal guard.

He checked his wristwatch. It was time to join the party.

HIS BLACKSUIT SAFELY stowed in the back of the Volkswagen microbus, Bolan wiped the cosmetics from his face with premoistened pads, slipped into the clothes he'd brought with him and drove up to the main gate.

Dressed in slacks, sport shirt and lightweight sport jacket, he stopped to answer the armed guard who had signaled to him.

"Your name?"

"Mike Belasko," Bolan said.

Running a finger down a typewritten list, the armed guard crossed off a name, then looked at Bolan again.

"Drive your van to the right. You'll find plenty of parking spaces there," he ordered.

As Bolan rounded the corner of the wide driveway, he could feel the guard's stare drilling into his back.

IT WAS TIME TO SHAKE a few trees and see what fell out, Bolan decided as he eased his way into the crowded mansion. His .44 caliber autopistol sat in the leather holster in the small of his back, and his Beretta 93-R in its shoulder rig. Because he would be shaking hands with strangers, Bolan had strapped the Ka-bar blade above his right ankle.

He was surprised that there had been no electronic security devices checking for hidden weapons at the entrance. But, looking at the burly, cold-faced men who kept staring at the guests, Bolan decided that Desmond was probably safe from most assailants.

Studying the faces of the guests, the warrior was surprised to see a mélange of skin colors among the well-dressed invitees. Whatever else he was, Harry Desmond wasn't a bigot.

Bolan felt a hand grab his shoulder. Reaching under his jacket for the shoulder rig, he turned. Jay Preston was standing there, a tall drink in his hand.

"Interesting mob," the young man commented. "The cream of Jo'burg."

The Executioner eased his grip on the Beretta.

"Mostly diplomats?"

"That, and politicians." He pointed out several cabinet ministers deep in discussion. "They're worried that they'll be unemployed after the government has had a chance to check into their personal finances. It takes a lot of money to keep terrorism alive. Most of it goes for arms and to bribe the right officials."

Bolan looked around the room. "Where's Sonda?"

Preston turned Bolan a few degrees. "Over there talking to an official from the African National Congress."

The young woman looked radiant. She had skillfully covered her facial bruises with makeup, and the dress she wore showed enough to make her desirable, without exposing the body beating she had taken.

Sonda saw the two men looking at her. She weaved her way through the crowds and joined them.

"Looks like you've recovered," Bolan commented.

"In more ways than you can imagine," she replied cryptically. She dug into her purse and took out a plastic-encased card, which she handed to Bolan.

"This counts. At least on Saturday."

He looked at the rectangular card. It was a pass that permitted him, as a member of the press, to go anywhere he wanted at the rally. Even next to the president.

"Thanks. I'll be there," he said, then remembered the newspaper story. "There was a shooting in Soweto last night. Four men were killed. All members of the Boasters gang."

"Uncle Reggie was a decent man. He hated people like the Boasters. What could be a more fitting tribute to him?"

"Four to one. Rough odds."

"I had a friend with me," the young woman replied, looking at Preston.

Bolan was about to ask about the death of Methabane. "I heard about what you did—"

She stopped him. "It's not over yet," she commented. Then, before he could question her, she turned and walked back to where the ANC official was chatting with Jay Preston.

Bolan turned his head and studied the faces of the various guests. For the most part they were people who were used to having money and power. They never dirtied their hands. They preferred letting their money and contacts get dirty instead.

He wondered if any of them had ever been forced to stand up and fight for what they believed. He doubted it.

A tall man in the uniform of a South African Defense Forces general was regaling several couples with anecdotes. Bolan suspected he had sent a great many young men to their deaths in foreign wars or local raids, without much concern, and then laid large wreaths to publicly mourn their loss for the benefit of television cameras.

Preston caught up with him halfway across the wide room.

"You looked bored," he commented, glancing at Bolan's face.

"I am," the Executioner admitted. "I just want to do what I came here for, and leave."

"Care to tell me what that is?"

Bolan was about to reply when a short, casually dressed man approached them, holding a drink in his hand. He glanced at the Executioner.

"You're going to make me look like a bad host if you don't have someone get you a drink." He smiled and held out a hand. "Hello. I'm Harry Desmond."

Bolan took the hand, then let it go without going through the motions of a handshake.

Desmond continued. "I know who you are," he said, glancing at Jay Preston. "American Embassy, aren't you?"

Preston nodded.

Desmond turned to Bolan. "And you?"

"Mike Belasko."

The host's eyes grew wider. "The infamous journalist!" He grabbed Bolan on the forearm. "There is someone who is dying to meet you."

Preston stayed behind and watched Desmond drag Bolan through the crowds. Then he turned and rejoined Sonda.

THE MINING MAGNATE KEPT searching for someone, then grinned when he saw a tall, Germanic-looking man in the uniform of a BOSS major.

Bringing Bolan within five feet of the other guest, he made the introductions. "Major Volksmann, this is Mike Belasko, the American journalist."

The BOSS officer started to hold his hand out, then saw the icy expression on Bolan's face and pulled it back.

"I'll leave you two alone to get better acquainted," Desmond said as he moved toward a man dressed in a double-breasted blazer and white linen pants.

"We keep just missing each other," Volksmann said lightly.

"I avoid coming into contact with anything that smells dead," Bolan replied.

Volksmann looked confused. "Explain, please."

"First you kill a black kid whose worst crime was writing speeches for a president who happens to be a black man. The man whose government pays your salary."

Volksmann smiled. "You must mean Kenneth Mgabe. Tragedy. One day we'll find the person responsible for his death."

Bolan ignored the glib explanation. "Then you grab his sister and order your men to torture her for information."

"I'm afraid you've got your facts wrong," Volksmann replied calmly. "A number of hard-working family men died trying to talk to those two."

"You ain't seen nothing yet," the Executioner snapped.

Volksmann didn't understand his slang. "Pardon?"

"You'll figure it out when you have to go job hunting. I hear they're looking for torturers in Iran."

"Nothing is guaranteed yet," the BOSS major warned. "Not everybody is happy to have a kaffir president."

"According to the election results, that's who the voters wanted."

"As a journalist, do you really trust anything you read in the papers?"

"Both of us know I'm not a reporter."

"What are you? A mercenary?"

"No. Someone you'll wish you never met."

Volksmann forced a weak smile on his face. "At least I don't think you will try to kill me in front of all these people."

"It crossed my mind."

Volksmann checked his wristwatch. "Well, back to work."

"Trying to replace all the arms shipments and recruits you've lost?"

Bolan knew he was baiting the BOSS officer. He hoped the major would drop his guard and snap something to incriminate himself publicly, and perhaps someone else at the party—like Desmond.

"It's a shame that Mozambique shipment got blown out of existence. Or that the Order of Death warehouse collapsed. Or the loss of that fishing trawler off Cape Town," Bolan added.

He could see Volksmann's body stiffen as he continued.

"I haven't mentioned the volunteer storm troopers who got killed in those incidents. The rat population of South Africa went down when they died." He paused. "How am I doing with those facts?"

"You are a dangerous man, Mr. Belasko." The BOSS officer lowered his voice. "At least you were until now."

"That's what happens when you get somebody angry. They can't stop what they're doing until they feel better."

"I take it you are still angry," the major replied.

"I'm a long way from feeling better," Bolan warned.

Volksmann stiffened, then said, "Excuse me. I must go."

He watched the BOSS major shove his way through the crowds. To get to the nearest telephone and call out the troops, Bolan suspected.

As soon as he took care of one more thing, he'd disappear.

Harry Desmond made it easier by joining him.

Looking around, the mining tycoon asked, "What happened to Major Volksmann?"

"He had to go back to work," Bolan replied.

"Typical policeman. Business always comes first," Desmond said casually. "Do you always think of work before pleasure?"

"Sometimes my work is a pleasure."

Desmond looked surprised, then replaced the expression with a broad grin.

"Good. Is there anything I can get you? Or anyone else you'd like to meet?" He waved his hand at the crowds. "They're all here."

Bolan looked around. "I don't see the new president here. I guess you forgot to invite him." He smiled. "Or maybe you thought he'd be dead by now."

Desmond's face turned pale as blood rushed from it.

Bolan checked his watch. "I've got a full day ahead tomorrow. Time for me to go home and get a good night's sleep."

He walked away from the still-stunned man and signaled for Preston to join him.

"Fireworks in ten minutes," he warned in a low voice. "Get the hell out of here."

"And miss all the fun? No way."

Preston patted the front of his jacket. There was a slight bulge.

Bolan wondered what the young agent was carrying as he led the way to the front door.

32

A haze covered the moon, making it difficult to distinguish the faces of the guests wandering around the veranda. Bolan checked carefully to make sure the BOSS major wasn't hiding in the shadows with a drawn handgun.

He had sent Preston to check out the driveway. The Agency man returned.

"Volksmann never came out, according to the guard," he reported in a low voice.

"Give it ten minutes and this place will be crawling with BOSS agents," Bolan warned, then pointed to the main steps. "Follow me."

The Executioner and the young CIA case officer strolled down the steps under the suspicious stares of two of Desmond's guards and made their way to the rented Volkswagen microbus and opened the rear door. Bolan unzipped one of the canvas carryalls and reached inside.

"Here," he said, handing Preston a 9 mm Uzi machine pistol and three clips for the weapon.

The young man dropped the magazines into a side jacket pocket.

Bolan turned to him. "What else are you carrying?"

Preston opened his jacket and handed the warrior his weapon, a .45 ACP Colt Commander, with modified three-dot sights.

Bolan approved of the agent's choice.

"Got any spare clips?"

Preston dug into his other pocket and tugged out a pair of magazines.

Bolan stared at him without expression. "Anything else?"

The young man thought the big man was joking. "Just a couple of hand grenades," he cracked.

The Executioner handed him a web belt and a pair of L-241 frag grenades.

As Bolan armed himself with a second 9 mm Uzi, spare magazines and a duplicate of the grenade-loaded belt, Preston asked, "What's the plan?"

"We take out the hardforce," the Executioner replied as he turned and led the way back to the main stairs.

Ahead he could see that the pair of guards had been joined by four more armed men and the large blond man who was Desmond's personal protector. The man cradled a Heckler & Koch MP-5 SMG in his arms.

They hadn't seen Bolan or the CIA agent yet. The Executioner turned to Preston. "We may have bigger troubles than I calculated."

The young man looked at the ex-soldiers standing at the top of the stairs.

"How about tossing a grenade?"

Bolan shook his head. "Too much risk of killing an innocent bystander." He made an instant decision. "We move the war away from the civilians."

He led the way around the garage and past the rear of the servants' quarters. A narrow path, overgrown with bushes and weeds, made their passage difficult.

Stomping down on the growth, Bolan worked his way to the northern end of the estate, followed by Preston.

The Executioner knew that the lack of lighting made it difficult for anyone to spot them without night-vision binoculars. Halfway across the rear end of the property, he stopped briefly and signaled for Preston to move up beside him.

Bolan pointed at the Tudor structure on his left. "We'll work our way back to the veranda in the shadows of the mansion," he whispered.

Preston nodded his agreement and kept close as the warrior crouched, then moved silently toward the front of the huge house, along the stone pillars that supported the veranda above their heads. In the distance they could hear the sounds of sirens.

"Volksmann's men are here," Bolan whispered.

Preston gripped his Uzi in his arms, looking ready for anyone who attacked him.

They could hear the major's voice, ordering his men to search the estate. Bolan didn't know how many had responded to Volksmann's call.

The Executioner kept moving forward, Preston close behind, then suddenly stopped and pointed upward.

"We'll take our stand up there," he whispered.

Slinging his Uzi, he reached up and grabbed one of the vertical stone bases that held the veranda railing in place. Straining his muscles, he pulled his body up until he could push himself between the widely spaced bases and onto the veranda.

As he stopped to catch his breath, Preston copied him and, breathing heavily, rested next to him.

He turned to Bolan. "What's next?"

"Wait for my signal," the warrior whispered as he stood. Pulling up his right pant leg, he freed the Ka-bar combat knife from the sheath and closed his fingers around the haft.

While Preston got to his feet, Bolan moved to the mansion wall and hid in the shadows. The Embassy officer moved behind him.

"Search for the American terrorist!" Volksmann shouted.

A young BOSS agent gripping an H&K Model 93 A-3 rifle moved onto the veranda, his eyes nervously darting in every direction.

Bolan waited until the man came within a few feet, then clamped a hand over his mouth and pulled the Ka-bar across the BOSS agent's throat. As rivulets of blood spurted from the severed arteries, the man's eyes glazed.

Gently the Executioner pulled him into the shadows and lowered his body to the floor of the veranda.

"Gert? Where the hell are you, Gert?" The voice had a raspy quality, the sound of a two-pack-a-day smoker.

The speaker came around the corner, his eyes searching for his partner. In his arms he carried a twin of the weapon the other BOSS agent had held. He studied the area carefully.

Something moved, and the hardman swung around to fire at the movement. Before he could, Bolan unleashed a pair of 9 mm rounds from the muffled Beretta 93-R. The slugs drilled through the man's breastbone and he dropped to the floor, blood oozing out of his mouth.

"Two down," Preston whispered.

"We don't know how many more came," Bolan reminded him in a whisper.

He signaled the young man to follow him as he resumed his movement along the side of the mansion. At the corner of the large structure, the warrior stopped. Then, holding his Beretta in front of him, he stepped out.

Volksmann stood to the side snapping orders to five husky armed men. He turned in Bolan's direction, but the Executioner had pulled back.

"Two of you around the corner," the major shouted, ignoring the people who had come outside to see what was going on.

Bolan gritted his teeth in frustration. Innocent bystanders. They limited his freedom to respond effectively.

The chosen pair of hardmen raised their H&K rifles and moved slowly to where Bolan and Preston were waiting. The two Americans held fire until the BOSS team rounded the corner.

Bolan's Beretta 93-R spit a 3-round burst at the nearer BOSS agent. The slugs shattered the facial bones of the security hit man and churned into his brain. The bloody mask moved a few feet toward the Executioner, then spun and fell backward.

Preston fired two rounds from his .45 ACP Colt Commander at the second hunter. The slugs carved into the man's chest, ripping open a wide cavity. Fractured ribs bent forward while frothy blood ran from the wide crevice onto the stone floor.

Bolan dropped the nearly empty clip and rammed home a fresh one. Now he was ready for whatever came next.

Volksmann ordered the rest of his men to attack. Reluctantly the remaining trio raised their H&K rifles and moved forward.

HARRY DESMOND HURRIED outside and herded the crowd of curious guests back into the living room.

"Just some hoodlums trying to break in," he said calmly. "The police are taking care of them."

Then he signaled Arthur, his personal guard, to join him at the glass doors to the veranda.

"I've ordered the men to find those two and take care of them quietly," Arthur stated in a low tone.

"Has Lucas Tsombe accepted the assignment?"

"Yes."

"The rally is still tomorrow?"

Arthur nodded.

Desmond shrugged. "I see no need to get involved in something that doesn't concern us," he said, then walked inside the mansion.

Arthur understood and called over one of his men.

"We stay out of it," he whispered when the man was at his side. "Pass the word."

Arthur and the guard got the message. The BOSS major was no longer useful. The mining magnate would make sure that street gangs would be blamed for the assault.

BOLAN SIGNALED Preston to stay where he was while the Executioner moved to the railing. He wanted to set up a cross fire for whoever came after them.

Side by side, the three remaining BOSS agents moved around the corner, their weapons probing the air in front of them.

They saw Bolan first. The gunner nearest the Executioner shifted the muzzle of his H&K assault rifle, but Bolan dodged to one side, unleashing a pair of slugs as he did.

Preston stepped out of the shadows, and, after choosing a target, emptied his carefully aimed Colt Commander. The heavy projectiles almost severed his adversary's head as they tore into his neck and throat, effectively taking him out of the play.

Panicked, the surviving gunner rammed his finger against the H&K trigger. Too terrified to take the time to aim, his wildly fired rounds tore into the brick wall of the mansion as Bolan dived to one side.

A ricocheting round from the H&K rifle churned through the soft flesh in Preston's shoulder. The impact knocked the CIA agent to the ground.

Bolan sent the last hardman to his whites-only paradise with three 9 mm parabellum rounds that shattered his stomach and exposed his hemorrhaging intestines.

Then he hurried to where the CIA man had fallen. Kneeling, he examined the wound. The slug had missed bone and large blood vessels, ripping only through soft flesh.

Preston tried to pull himself up.

"It's almost over," Bolan told him. "Take it easy."

Grimacing from pain, the CIA officer lowered his head and tried to relax while the Executioner crouched and checked the still forms on the ground.

Too many friends had died because they assumed an enemy was dead, not just badly injured. Assured the BOSS attackers were dead, Bolan stood—and felt the muzzle of a handgun poking his neck.

"In the end you lose," Volksmann commented cynically. "And the kaffir you seem to love so much will join you soon."

"No," another voice said softly. It belonged to a woman. Bolan could hear the muffled sound of a silenced gun unleashing a round.

Volksmann groaned and shuddered.

Bolan spun out of the way before an involuntary reaction of the BOSS major's trigger finger released a slug into his neck. He turned and saw the cold expression on Sonda Mgabe's face as she kept pulling the trigger of her 9 mm H&K P-7 M-8.

Volksmann head snapped back with each round she fired. Finally the hammer of her H&K hit bare metal and the major crumpled to the ground.

She stared at Bolan with glistening eyes and began to sob softly. He took her arm and steered her to where Preston was resting.

She ran to his side and kneeled, letting the young Agency officer pat her arm with his uninjured hand.

Desmond came out of the house, followed closely by Arthur. He looked around at the bodies and turned to the bodyguard.

"Call somebody about them," he ordered. Then he saw Preston. Desmond looked at Bolan. "One of the guests is head of surgery at the Johannesburg Hospital. I'll ask him to have a look."

Bolan said nothing. There wasn't much to say. He ignored the small man and sat on the ground, his back against one of the stone support columns. Returning his Beretta to its shoulder holster, he stared at the bodies around him. What was left of Volksmann's face stared back at him.

He remembered the major's comment only minutes earlier: *In the end you lose.*

Bolan shook his head. "In the end we all lose," he told the BOSS officer's corpse.

The dead security officer had no reply.

On Saturday morning crowds began to arrive at dawn. By nine the stands at Soccer City were almost full. Long lines of people, both blacks and whites, waited patiently at more than a dozen entrances for their turn to enter the huge sports stadium.

There was a festive feeling flowing from the mass of humanity outside the stadium. For many this would be the first time they had a chance to see the president in person.

A smaller, exuberant crowd waited at the curb for the arrival of the president's limousine. Each time the constables ordered them away, the people moved back, then returned to the curb.

Mack Bolan, his press card hanging from a cord around his neck, studied the faces of those at the curb, but saw no one who looked suspicious. He had seen pictures of Lucas Tsombe, and nobody nearby bore even a passing resemblance.

Bolan was about to move inside when he heard police sirens approach the stadium. He decided that it wouldn't hurt to delay his entrance a few minutes.

Four police motorcyles escorted a long black limousine to the curb. Two smaller cars pulled up behind it.

Four men wearing business suits, their expressions grim, exited the first of the two smaller vehicles and stared suspiciously at the crowds of people pushing toward the limousine.

The crowd began to chant, the sound growing in volume. They kept shouting the president's name, waving posters and dancing in joy.

Another grim-faced man climbed from the second car, followed by a woman in a conservative dress. Sonda Mgabe's expression was cold and businesslike.

Bolan had seen others who wore the same expression on duty—the agents of the White House Secret Service detail when they walked alongside the presidential limousine.

He wondered if Sonda still had mixed loyalties.

The group moved as one to the limousine and tried to push the crowds away from the rear door. The growing number of spectators continued their exuberant chanting.

Bolan had joined the crowds at six that morning, standing on the side and studying them as they passed into the open-air stadium.

Whatever feelings he still had about the previous night were set aside. The success of his mission depended on whether the president lived through today to see tomorrow, and whether those who would have him killed did not.

Bolan carefully watched as one of the bodyguards opened the rear door of the limousine and Jay Preston emerged. His plaster-encased arm was supported by a cloth sling.

The CIA operative saw Bolan and nodded, then turned back and offered his good hand to the person inside.

A tall, gray-haired black man in a smartly tailored business suit let the young American help him get out. Then he looked at the crowd and waved.

The crowds became hysterical with joy at seeing him.

Still, Bolan had a gut feeling something was wrong. He stared at Sonda and wondered if it was her. As the president moved through the large crowds, the feeling wouldn't go away. He focused his gaze on the people pressing toward the black leader.

The team of bodyguards moved with the tall, well-dressed black man, scanning the crowds as they did. Sonda walked by the man's side, turning her head constantly and staring suspiciously at everybody.

Some instinct told the Executioner that Sonda wasn't the problem. It was someone else. But nobody made an overt move at the tall black man.

Bolan was about to turn away and go inside the sports arena when he saw a short, stout white man with a white beard push his way through the crowds.

The man was shouting something unintelligible. Bolan stared at the shouter's hand. He was clenching a 9 mm SIG-Sauer P-226, and shaking with rage, he raised the weapon.

The warrior propelled himself forward, thrusting people aside.

The bearded man screamed something about his dead son and the kaffirs, and shoved the weapon in the president's face. His hand was trembling as he started to pull the trigger.

Suddenly Sonda Mgabe shouldered the president aside and lunged at the gunman.

The crazed man jerked the trigger, and a hollowpoint round drilled into the young woman's chest. Jay Preston rushed to her side as the killer turned to escape.

The still-hysterical gunman pointed the pistol at the terrified crowd around him. Alarmed by the sudden explosion of violence, people rushed out of his path.

He began to run and came face-to-face with Bolan. The Executioner didn't hesitate. A trio of slugs from the business end of his Beretta punched into the shooter's chest, spraying the crowd around him with dark red life fluid.

Police constables shoved the horrified crowd back and surrounded the body of the attacker.

One of them, a sallow-faced Afrikaner, recognized him.

"It's Jan Gruber of the AWB," he told one of the other policemen on duty. "He must have been *krank.*"

"Ja," the second constable agreed. "I heard he's been out of his mind since his son was murdered."

Bolan moved to where Sonda Mgabe lay. Jay Preston sat on the ground, cradling her head in his lap.

He looked up, stunned by the violence, and asked, "Why?"

Bolan didn't have an answer.

The angry lieutenant in charge of the constables at the stadium pointed a .45 ACP Colt Double Eagle pistol the Executioner's head. "You're under arrest," he said grimly.

The president of South Africa stepped in front of Mack Bolan and glared at the uniformed police official.

"He's with me," he said quietly.

The police commander grumbled but moved away to deal with the hysterical crowds.

"Thank you," the tall black man said to Bolan, then let the rest of the bodyguard group walk him into the stadium.

Bolan followed a few steps behind. There was nothing he could do for either the dead young woman or Jay Preston. And there was still the rumored black assassin to find inside the stadium.

Lucas Tsombe had spent the night in the stadium. Hiding in a small storeroom, he had wrapped himself in a blanket he'd found in an electrical locker and slept on the floor.

It was easier than going home and trying to get back into Soccer City in the morning, especially with police constables who knew his face guarding the giant sports complex.

Checking that nobody was observing him, Tsombe opened the electrical locker and took out the gun case. Assembling the long-range rifle took less than ten minutes. He grabbed one of the magazines in the metal cabinet and fitted it into the weapon, then jacked a round into the chamber.

Sighting the gun was simple. Through the scope he could see clearly across the wide arena. He focused on the speaker's platform, locking the scope onto where the president would stand.

He had taken the precaution of stacking a number of sandbags to stabilize the speakers. Using them to steady the SR-25, he knew he was ready.

Tsombe heard police sirens outside the stadium, which heralded the president's arrival. In less than a half hour, the hit man would be ready to leave Soccer City.

He had worked out an escape route—down the stairs to the upper-level seats, then he would work his way around to the opposite side and let the crowd, shocked by the killing, carry him outside. His Mercedes-Benz was safely parked several streets away.

Tsombe had a round-trip airline ticket to Angola in his jacket pocket. It was under a false name, but one he had invented for the fake passport he'd purchased several years earlier. In his business, it was smarter to be prepared to run than try to stay and fight.

His money had been transferred to a bank in Bahrain, so he had more than enough funds available to live well until he could go back into business someplace else.

There was only one stop he had to make before he boarded the plane to Angola. The Sunnyside Hotel in Parktown, where the huge blond man said he'd meet him with the rest of his fee.

The commotion outside brought him back to the present. Somebody had fired a gun; he could hear the crack of cartridge powder exploding.

He hoped no one had already killed the president. It would be impossible to collect his payment if someone else was blamed for the shooting.

The sudden sound of music pouring from the huge speakers around Tsombe startled him. Then he realized that meant the president was entering the stadium. He leaned over and peered through the scope. The seats near the speaker stand were still empty, but he could discern figures walking toward them from one of the stadium entrances.

Tsombe got himself into a more comfortable position and leaned into the SR-25. He wanted to be ready.

MACK BOLAN DECLINED the invitation to sit with the presidential party. Waving the press badge at the tall black man, he apologized. "I want to move around."

His Beretta restored to its holster, the Executioner moved out, his narrowed gaze searching the upper level of the stadium. He knew an assassin was hiding someplace up there. But where? All he could do was conduct a painstaking search and hope to find the gunman before he could get off a shot.

As Bolan climbed the incline to the upper levels of the giant arena, he looked at as many people as he could, hoping to spot Lucas Tsombe. According to Jay Preston's informant, that was who had been hired to do the killing.

He scanned every possible hiding place, even rest rooms and storage areas.

His inspection tour finally led to the top level of the giant structure. As he moved along a narrow path, he saw a short flight of stairs ahead, access barred by a heavy-wire door.

A uniformed stadium guard leaned against a nearby wall.

Bolan nodded to him and asked, "What's up there?"

"The speakers."

"Anybody working on them?"

"Nobody's allowed upstairs," the guard snapped.

Bolan flashed his press badge. "I'm allowed to go anywhere I want."

The guard read the press card carefully, then, showing his annoyance, growled, "Nothing up there worth seeing."

"Open the gate."

Reluctantly the man complied. Bolan, ignoring the hostile looks, climbed the stairs.

Loud marching music started to blast from the speakers. If an assassin was hiding up here, he was either stone-deaf or would be soon.

Bolan scanned the area, deciding nobody was up there. Then he turned his head and glanced out into the open stadium. He could see all the way to where the president stood in front of a bank of microphones. This would be the ideal place for a sniper.

The Executioner decided to search the area more closely. Moving around the piles of sandbags that held the speakers steady, he wondered where an assassin could hide.

A glint of metal caught his eye. Not sure what had caused it, he eased his Beretta out of the shoulder rig and moved toward the reflection.

A long-range rifle rested on a stack of sandbags. Bolan looked around for the shooter.

A dark figure jumped out at him from behind one of the six-foot-high speakers. The Executioner tried to twist to one side, but Lucas Tsombe wrapped his arms around Bolan's neck and began to choke him.

He tried to point his Beretta at the Boaster chieftain, but the gangster tightened his choke-hold.

Struggling to free himself, the Executioner caught his foot on a speaker cable and fell backward. Tsombe fell on him and tore the weapon from his grip. Then he wrapped his hands around the warrior's throat again and pressed his thumbs into the carotid artery.

Bolan tried to tear the assassin's hands from his throat. He could almost feel the blood flow stopping, and unless he freed himself, he'd be dead soon.

In desperation he pulled his hands down to his waist and pushed at a jacket sleeve. The Ka-bar blade was locked into place underneath it by a catch in its leather sheath. Bolan tugged at the knife with his fingertips and finally freed it. Consciousness was rapidly slipping away. He knew that if he waited any longer he wouldn't have the strength to fight back.

There was no time left to do anything fancier than survive.

Bolan wrapped his right hand around the haft and rammed the blade into Tsombe's mouth. The gang leader screamed with pain, but his screeching was drowned out by the now-thundering martial music.

Bolan pulled out the blade and slashed it across Tsombe's throat. The leader of the Boasters tried to scream again, but his vocal cords had been slashed at the same time as his carotid artery. His lifeless body collapsed onto the Executioner. Shoving the body away, Bolan pulled himself to his feet.

Reaching down, he picked up the long-range rifle. An envelope filled with money fell out of the dead man's pocket. Bolan glanced at the printing on the envelope, and he wasn't surprised at the company name printed in the upper-left corner.

He'd turn the gun and the envelope with money over to the bodyguards as he left the stadium. They'd know what to do with them.

He picked up his blade and handgun and returned them to their carriers. It was time for him to go home. He'd call Brognola to make the arrangements. He knew that the newly alerted bodyguards would guard their charge even more closely until the terrorist groups and their backers were exposed and destroyed.

As he walked down the steps, Bolan saw the guard stare in shock at his bloody hands. It didn't matter what the man thought. The warrior was too tired to care.

Bolan stopped and looked at the well-dressed man at the microphones. He was quoting from a poem written by an Afrikaner. The warrior had seen the poem quoted in the airline magazine during the flight to South Africa.

As he remembered, it was titled, "The Child Who Was Shot Dead," or something like that. He thought of Sonda Mgabe and her sacrifice at the last minute. The poem was an appropriate epitaph to the young black woman.

One of the bodyguards was standing near an exit, sneaking a smoke. As he passed him, Bolan handed over the rifle and the envelope. He explained briefly, then kept walking.

Exiting Soccer City, Mack Bolan thought of a popular song of the sixties about "the times they're a-changin'."

Not everything, he reminded himself. He was sure that Desmond would survive the scandal, and that he and the bigots would be around for a long time. But he had stopped them for now.

Maybe, before they could get together again and try to shove South Africa back into the Dark Ages, the people would find out that it was easier to live together than kill one another, and they would stand shoulder to shoulder against the hate brokers.

He knew it wouldn't be easy for a whole country to change, not overnight, not after all the years of oppression.

But at least there was now hope that things would get better for everyone.